The Sea Train Chronicles

The Call of the Waves

By

Darian Storm

Dedicated to my kids and niece:

~ Abdiel, David, Ava and Vivianna ~

Let all your dreams come true. Never lose sight of them and only stop when you have reached them. From there, set sights on new heights, as it is there were true adventure, courage, and strength would be found.

Table of Contents

Part I:

Life in Aeloria, it's only port city (Dave's Landing), its people, the general ambiance, and our main characters.

Chapter I:
Introduction to Aeloria

Aeloria was a gem in the vast ocean, an island paradise where emerald jungles kissed azure shores. Aeloria's Island is also a place of mystical beauty and profound natural wonder, located in the heart of the Azure Sea. The island is not only renowned for its lush jungles and pristine shores but also for its unique geographical features and diverse ecosystems.

Aeloria's Island is situated in the central part of the Azure Sea, a vast and deep body of water that lies between the continents of Eldoria to the north and Calandria to the south. The Azure Sea is known for its clear, turquoise waters, rich marine life, and numerous islands, of which Aeloria is one of the most prominent.

The island's exact coordinates place it roughly at 15°N latitude and 45°W longitude. This location grants Aeloria's Island a tropical climate characterized by warm temperatures year-round and abundant rainfall, especially during the monsoon season. The island's position also makes it a crucial waypoint for sailors and traders navigating the Azure Sea, contributing to its rich cultural and economic interactions with other regions.

Aeloria's Island spans approximately 25,289 square miles, making it one of the larger islands in the Azure Sea. The island's terrain is highly varied, featuring everything from dense jungles and rugged mountains to serene beaches and fertile plains. This geographical diversity supports a wide range of flora and fauna, many of which are unique to the island.

The Central Highlands

The heart of Aeloria's Island is dominated by the Central Highlands, a range of mountains and hills that rise steeply from the surrounding lowlands. The highest peak, Mount Eldoria, stands at 6,200 feet and is often shrouded in mist, giving it a mystical appearance. The Central Highlands are covered in dense forests and are home to numerous waterfalls and rivers originating in the mountains and flowing down to the coast.

The highlands are also rich in minerals and gemstones, and small mining communities, like the Dwarves, have established themselves in the more accessible areas. These communities are known for their skill in extracting and crafting precious stones, which are highly valued in trade.

The Eastern Shore and the Land of the Giant Crabs

The eastern shore of Aeloria's Island is characterized by its pristine beaches and rocky outcrops. This area, known as the Land of the Giant Crabs, is famous for its enormous crustaceans, which can often be seen foraging along the shoreline. The beaches here are composed of fine, white sand, and the waters are clear and calm, making it a popular spot for swimming and snorkeling.

The rocky outcrops and tide pools along the eastern shore provide habitats for a variety of marine life, including colorful fish, sea anemones, and starfish. Coral reefs just offshore teem with life, offering a stunning display of underwater biodiversity. Here is where the legendary Fish people live, and they keep watch over one of Aeloria's greatest treasures.

The Western Jungles

The western part of the island is dominated by vast jungles that are both beautiful and treacherous. These jungles are home to a myriad of plant and animal species, many of which have yet to be documented by naturalists. The jungle canopy is incredibly dense, with towering trees that create a thick, green roof over the forest floor.

The western jungles are also home to many of the island's mystical creatures, such as the Drakkenbeast and the Shadow Panther. These creatures add an element of danger to the jungle, and only the most skilled and brave explorers venture into its depths.

The Southern Plains

The southern part of Aeloria's Island features fertile plains that are used for agriculture by the island's inhabitants. The Elven's ("at least most of them") call this part of the island their home. These plains are crisscrossed by rivers and streams that provide essential irrigation for crops. The soil is rich and supports a variety of crops, including grains, fruits, and vegetables.

Small villages and farming communities (some humans and others half-breed) dot the southern plains, their inhabitants living in harmony with the land (and with each other). These communities are known for their hospitality and strong traditions of farming and craftsmanship.

The Northern Cliffs

The northern coast of Aeloria's Island is defined by dramatic cliffs that rise sharply from the sea. These cliffs, carved by centuries of wind and waves, offer breathtaking views of the Azure Sea. The cliffs are dotted with caves and grottos, some of which are rumored to hold ancient treasures and relics.

The northern cliffs are also home to colonies of seabirds, whose cries fill the air. The cliffs are a challenging but rewarding destination for climbers and adventurers seeking to explore the island's rugged beauty.

"Dave's Landing is located between the southern plains and the northern cliffs." "More on that later" (sighting).

Chapter II:
The Ecosystems of Aeloria's Island

Aeloria's Island supports a diverse array of ecosystems, each with its own unique flora and fauna. This biodiversity is a testament to the island's varied terrain and climate, which provides a range of habitats for different species.

The Rainforests

The rainforests of Aeloria's Island are a lush and vibrant ecosystem, teeming with life. These forests are characterized by their high rainfall and dense vegetation, which create a humid and sheltered environment. The canopy is home to numerous bird species, including parrots, toucans, and eagles, while insects, reptiles, and small mammals inhabit the forest floor.

The rainforests are also rich in medicinal plants and herbs, many of which are used by the island's inhabitants for healing and wellness. The knowledge of these plants is passed down through generations, and herbalists are highly respected members of the community (mainly by those with great knowledge of the jungle and brave enough to adventure in it for them).

The Coastal Ecosystems

The coastal areas of Aeloria's Island include sandy beaches, rocky shores, and coral reefs. These ecosystems are home to a wide variety of marine life, from fish and crustaceans to sea turtles and dolphins. The coral reefs (in particular) are a hotspot of biodiversity, with their vibrant colors and intricate structures providing shelter and food for many species.

The shores of Aeloria's Island are a stark contrast to the dense jungle. Pristine, white-sand beaches stretch for miles, lapped by the clear, turquoise waters of the ocean. The coastline is dotted with hidden coves and secluded bays, each one more beautiful than the last. Coral reefs just offshore are home to a dazzling array of marine life, from colorful fish to graceful sea turtles. The waters around the island are warm and inviting, perfect for swimming, snorkeling, and exploring.

The coastal ecosystems are also crucial for the island's economy, as fishing and tourism are significant sources of income. Sustainable practices are emphasized to ensure that these natural resources are preserved for future generations.

The Wetlands

Scattered throughout the island, especially in the low-lying areas, are wetlands that provide vital habitats for a range of species. These wetlands include marshes, swamps, and mangrove forests, which act as nurseries for fish and amphibians and provide bird nesting sites.

The wetlands are also crucial for water filtration and flood control, helping to maintain the island's delicate ecological balance. The mangrove forests, with their complex root systems, are particularly important in protecting the coastline from erosion and storm surges.

The Highland Ecosystems

The highlands and mountainous regions of Aeloria's Island have their own unique ecosystems characterized by cooler temperatures and different vegetation. These areas are home to hardy plants that can withstand the rocky terrain and thin soil, as well as animals adapted to the cooler climate.

The rivers and streams that originate in the highlands are vital for the island's water supply, providing fresh water to the lower regions and supporting diverse aquatic life. These waterways are also a source of hydroelectric power harnessed by the island's inhabitants to provide sustainable energy.

Chapter III:
The Jungle of Aeloria's Island

Aeloria's Jungle: Beauty and Dangers

Aeloria's Jungle is a captivating expanse of verdant foliage and ancient trees, where every step taken feels like a journey into a land of enchantment and peril. The jungle is a living, breathing entity that extends from the highlands to the southern plains at the center of the island. The jungle's dense canopy of leaves and vines creates a world of shadows and light, where the air seems to hum with magic. This lush paradise, however, is also fraught with dangers, as it harbors some of the most mystical and formidable creatures known to exist.

The Beauty of Aeloria's Jungle

Aeloria's Jungle is a place of unparalleled natural beauty. The towering trees, some reaching hundreds of feet into the sky, form a thick canopy that filters sunlight into a soft, green glow. This canopy is a mosaic of different shades of green, interspersed with bursts of color from flowering plants and fruits that dangle like jewels from the branches. The jungle floor is a rich tapestry of ferns, mosses, and wildflowers, creating a lush, green carpet underfoot.

The flora of Aeloria's Jungle is incredibly diverse and often magical. Bioluminescent plants glow softly in the dark, illuminating the paths with an ethereal light. Flowers of every color imaginable bloom in profusion, some with petals that shimmer like precious gems. Rare and potent herbs grow in hidden groves, their properties known only to the island's inhabitants. The trees themselves are often imbued with magic, their wood possessing unique properties that make them highly sought after by craftsmen and mages alike.

Giant ferns, some as tall as small trees, create a prehistoric atmosphere, while delicate orchids bloom in the most unexpected places, their vibrant colors standing out against the greenery. Vines and creepers twist and climb, forming natural arches and curtains of leaves. Some plants have evolved bioluminescence, casting an ethereal glow at night and illuminating the paths with their soft light.

Water is a constant presence in the jungle, with streams and rivers winding their way through the landscape. These waterways are crystal clear, their surfaces reflecting the vibrant colors of the surrounding foliage. Waterfalls cascade down rocky cliffs, their mist creating rainbows in the sunlight. Hidden deep within the jungle, pools of water provide a serene contrast to the surrounding wilderness, their surfaces often covered in delicate water lilies.

The air in Aeloria's Jungle is thick with the scent of flowers and the earthy aroma of damp leaves. The sounds of the jungle are a symphony of life; the birds' calls, the insects' chirping, and the leaves' rustling create a constant, lively background. Every now and then, the distant roar of a waterfall or the call of a larger animal adds a dramatic note to this natural orchestra.

The fauna of Aeloria's Island is equally diverse and wondrous. Colorful birds with intricate plumage flit through the trees, their songs creating a symphony of sound. Monkeys swing from branch to branch, chattering and playing in the treetops. Exotic animals, both large and small, roam the jungle floor. Some of these creatures are found nowhere else in the world, and their unique adaptations allow them to thrive in this magical environment.

Aeloria's Island is also home to several ancient ruins, remnants of a long-lost civilization. These ruins are scattered throughout the jungle and along the coast, their origins shrouded in mystery. Crumbling temples, overgrown with vines, hint at a time when powerful magic was commonplace. Inscriptions and carvings on the stone walls tell stories of gods and heroes, and hidden chambers hold untold treasures and ancient artifacts. These ruins are a source of fascination and adventure for those visiting and living on the island, offering glimpses into a forgotten past.

The Dangers of Aeloria's Jungle

Beneath its breathtaking beauty, Aeloria's Jungle conceals many dangers. The dense foliage and towering trees provide the perfect hiding places for numerous predators and mystical beasts. Travelers must tread carefully, for the jungle is as treacherous as it is beautiful.

One of the most significant dangers in the jungle is the presence of carnivorous plants. Often indistinguishable from their harmless counterparts, these plants have evolved to trap and consume unsuspecting prey. Some have large, sticky leaves that close around anything that touches them, while others use sweet-smelling nectar to lure their victims into their deadly grasp. These plants are often found in the darker, more secluded parts of the jungle, where their prey is less likely to escape.

The jungle is also home to numerous venomous creatures. Snakes, with their iridescent scales and hypnotic eyes, slither silently through the underbrush, ready to strike at any moment. Spiders, some as large as a human hand, weave their webs between the trees, their venomous bites capable of paralyzing their prey. Even some of the more innocuous-looking insects carry venom that can cause severe pain or even death.

Mystical and Dangerous Beasts

Among the most formidable inhabitants of Aeloria's Jungle are the mystical and dangerous beasts that roam its depths. These creatures, often shrouded in legend and mystery, add an element of the supernatural to the jungle's many perils.

The Drakkenbeast

One of the most feared creatures in the jungle is the Drakkenbeast, a massive, dragon-like creature with scales that shimmer like emeralds in the sunlight. The Drakkenbeast is known for its fierce temperament and incredible strength. It has powerful jaws lined with razor-sharp teeth, and its claws can slice through the thickest tree trunks. The Drakkenbeast is a solitary creature, preferring to hunt alone and ambush its prey from the shadows. Despite its fearsome reputation, sightings of the Drakkenbeast are rare, as it tends to avoid areas frequented by humans. "Some lucky or unlucky individuals have placed the Drakkenbeast territory somewhere by the ruins of the lost history that lay closest to the heart of the jungle by the feet of Mount Eldoria.

The Shadow Panther

Another mystical beast that calls the jungle home is the Shadow Panther. This elusive predator is known for its ability to blend seamlessly into the darkness, becoming nearly invisible in the shadows. The Shadow Panther is a master of stealth, stalking its prey silently and striking with deadly precision. Its eyes, which glow with an eerie blue light, are often the only indication of its presence. Legends say that the Shadow Panther is a guardian of the jungle, punishing those who seek to exploit its resources.

The Serpent of the Deep

Near the largest rivers and lakes, the Serpent of the Deep dwells in the deeper parts of the jungle. This massive, snake-like creature is said to be as long as a river and as old as the jungle itself. The Serpent of the Deep is a creature of legend, believed to possess powerful magic and wisdom. It is often associated with water, and sightings of the Serpent are considered both a blessing and a warning. Those who respect the jungle and its inhabitants are said to be protected by the Serpent, while those who seek to harm it are met with its wrath. She is the guardian of the entrance of the legendary dungeon located on the eastern side of Mount Eldoria. Legend has it that if you encounter the Serpent and pass her trial, she will take the fortunate one to the entrance and furnish upon him the power, magic, and wisdom needed to reach the ultimate price. The price that lies at the heart of the dungeon.

The East Shore and the Land of the Giant Crabs

The east shore of Aeloria's Island is a stark contrast to the dense jungle. Here, the land meets the sea in a series of pristine beaches and rocky outcrops. This area is known as the Land of the Giant Crabs, named for the enormous crustaceans that inhabit the shoreline.

The Giant Crabs

The Giant Crabs of Aeloria's Island are formidable creatures, with shells as hard as rock and pincers powerful enough to crush bone. These crabs can grow to be as large as small boats, and their presence on the shore is both a spectacle and a danger. The crabs are generally peaceful, spending their days foraging for food and basking in the sun. However, they can become aggressive if threatened, and their sheer size and strength make them formidable opponents.

The shells of the Giant Crabs are highly prized for their durability and are often used by the island's inhabitants to create armor and tools. The crabs themselves are considered a delicacy, and hunting them is a dangerous but rewarding endeavor.

The Legend of the Fish People

Beyond the shore, in the waters surrounding Aeloria's Island, lies another mystery: the legend of the Fish People. According to ancient tales, the Fish People are a race of amphibious beings who inhabit the underwater caves and coral reefs off the east coast of the island.

Origins and Appearance

The Fish People are said to be descendants of an ancient civilization that once thrived on the island. According to legend, these people made a pact with the sea gods, gaining the ability to live both on land and underwater. Over time, they adapted to their new environment, developing gills, webbed hands and feet, and scales that shimmered like pearls.

The Fish People are described as being both beautiful and eerie, with eyes that glow in the dark and voices that sound like the call of the sea. They are believed to be highly intelligent and possess advanced knowledge of magic and technology. Legends talk about how they used to operate the Sea Train and help those who managed to gain the right to set foot on its decks.

Interaction with Islanders

The relationship between the Fish People and the inhabitants of Aeloria's Island is complex. While some stories speak of cooperation and mutual respect, others tell of conflict and mistrust, "but that was so long ago, the island's current inhabitants have forgotten about them all." The Fish People are said to guard their underwater domain fiercely, and those who venture too close to their territory without permission are rarely seen again.

Despite this, there are tales of encounters between the Fish People and the islanders, where knowledge and goods were exchanged. The Fish People are believed to have shared their knowledge of the sea, teaching the islanders how to navigate the waters and harness the power of the ocean.

The Sacred Caves

One of the most significant aspects of the legend of the Fish People is the existence of the Sacred Caves. These underwater caverns are said to be the heart of the Fish People's civilization, a place of great power and mystery. The Sacred Caves are believed to be filled with ancient artifacts, magical relics, and the remains of a lost civilization.

Accessing the Sacred Caves is said to be incredibly difficult, requiring both magical and physical prowess. The caves are protected by powerful enchantments and guarded by the Fish People, who only allow those deemed worthy to enter. It is said that those who do gain access to the caves are granted great knowledge and power, but at a significant cost. Beyond the caves lies Aeloria's fourth and last mystical beast, the Sea Serpent, "But that's a story for a later time."

Conclusion

Aeloria's Jungle and the east shore of Aeloria's Island are places of unparalleled beauty and danger. With its lush foliage, vibrant flora, and diverse fauna, the jungle is a place of wonder and enchantment. However, it is also home to many dangers, from venomous creatures to mystical beasts like the Drakkenbeast, the Shadow Panther, and the Serpent of the Deep.

The east shore, known as the Land of the Giant Crabs, offers a different kind of danger and beauty. The Giant Crabs that inhabit this area are formidable creatures, and the legend of the Fish People adds an element of mystery and intrigue to the region.

Together, these elements create a rich and captivating tapestry of life, magic, and legend, making Aeloria's Island a place of endless adventure and discovery. Whether one is drawn to the beauty of the jungle, the thrill of encountering mystical beasts, or the mystery of the Fish People, Aeloria's Island offers something for everyone, promising a journey unlike any other.

Chapter IV:
Dave's Landing

Introduction to Dave's Landing

In the heart of the mystical land of Aeloria lies Dave's Landing, the only port city that serves as the bustling center of trade and adventure. The city is a vibrant tapestry of cobbled streets, bustling markets, and grand ships docking from lands afar. Its people are filled with dreams of discovering uncharted territories, seeking hidden treasures, and forging lifelong friendships.

Dave's Landing

Dave's Landing is a unique and vibrant settlement located on the shores of an expansive and serene bay. The bay is nestled between the Northern Cliffs and the Southern Plains. The settlement is named after its founder, Captain Dave, a legendary explorer known for his compassionate leadership and vision of a harmonious community. This small town has grown into a bustling, multicultural haven where people from all walks of life coexist in peace and prosperity.

The heart of Dave's Landing is its marketplace. In this colorful and dynamic space, traders from distant lands gather to exchange goods and stories. The air is filled with the rich aromas of exotic spices, the sounds of various languages, and the sights of diverse cultural artifacts. Stalls and shops line the cobblestone streets, each one a testament to the town's inclusive nature. Here, you can find handcrafted jewelry from the Elven artisans, intricate tapestries woven by the Dwarves, and vibrant textiles dyed by the Humans.

The architecture of Dave's Landing is a reflection of its multicultural identity. Buildings are constructed in a blend of styles, each influenced by the traditions of the different races that call this place home. Elven spires with delicate carvings stand alongside sturdy Dwarven stonework and elegant human townhouses with large windows and airy balconies. This architectural tapestry creates a visually stunning and unique environment, symbolizing the unity and cooperation of the community.

One of the key aspects of life in Dave's Landing is the emphasis on mutual respect and understanding. They have adapted to the island's unique environment, living in harmony with nature and each other. The town council, which governs the settlement, is composed of representatives from each race, ensuring that all voices are heard and decisions are made collectively. Festivals and cultural events are a regular occurrence, providing opportunities for everyone to share their traditions, music, dance, and cuisine. These celebrations foster a sense of belonging and appreciation for the rich tapestry of cultures present in the town.

Education in Dave's Landing is highly valued, with schools offering a curriculum that includes the histories, languages, and arts (magic and swordsmanship) of all races.

This holistic approach to learning ensures that the younger generations grow up with an appreciation for diversity and an understanding of the importance of living in harmony. Children of different races attend classes together, forging lifelong friendships and breaking down any potential barriers of prejudice. The people have also developed a deep connection to the magic of the land. Many are skilled in various forms of magic, from elemental manipulation to healing spells. This magical knowledge is passed down through generations (mostly by the Elven's, but not out of reach for others who seek such knowledge). Normally, the elders teach the young in traditions that date back centuries. The inhabitants use their magic to protect and nurture the environment, ensuring that the delicate balance of nature is maintained.

The natural environment surrounding Dave's Landing is equally breathtaking. The settlement is nestled between lush forests and the tranquil bay, offering stunning views and ample opportunities for outdoor activities. The people of Dave's Landing have a deep respect for nature, and efforts are made to preserve the beauty and health of the environment. Parks and gardens are scattered throughout the town, providing green spaces for relaxation and recreation.

The bay itself is a hub of activity, with fishing boats and trade ships constantly coming and going. The waters are teeming with marine life, and sustainable fishing practices ensure that the bounty of the sea remains plentiful for future generations. The harbor is a lively place where sailors and merchants share tales of their adventures and exchange news from distant lands.

Dave's Landing is also a place of spiritual significance. Sacred groves, hidden in the depths of the jungle, serve as places of worship and meditation (for those who know the safe way to reach them). Here, the islanders connect with the spirits of the land, seeking guidance and wisdom. Rituals and ceremonies are an integral part of life on the island, celebrating the changing seasons, the cycles of the moon, and the bond between the people and nature.

Healthcare in Dave's Landing is advanced, with a hospital that integrates the medicinal knowledge of all races. Elven herbal remedies, Dwarven surgical techniques, and Human holistic practices are all utilized to provide the best care for everyone. This collaborative approach to medicine has led to significant advancements and a high standard of health for the community.

Dave's Landing is also a place of innovation and creativity. Artisans and inventors thrive in this environment, where new ideas are encouraged and supported. Workshops and studios can be found throughout the town, where craftspeople work on their creations and share their skills with apprentices from different races. The fusion of various cultural influences often results in groundbreaking inventions and beautiful works of art.

The spirit of cooperation extends to all aspects of life in Dave's Landing. Disputes are resolved through dialogue and mediation, with an emphasis on finding common ground and understanding each other's perspectives. This approach has created a peaceful and stable society where crime is low, and trust among the residents is high.

Chapter V:
Dave's Landing: The General Ambiance of Its People

Dave's Landing is a remarkable settlement known for its vibrant atmosphere and harmonious way of life. This town is a beacon of multicultural coexistence, where people from various backgrounds, races, and cultures live together in peace and mutual respect. The spirit of the community is evident in every aspect of life, from the bustling market to the joyous festivities that unite everyone in celebration. The two main areas at Dave's Landing are its port and the market. The seaport of Dave's Landing is a bustling center of commerce and trade, with a constant flow of goods moving in and out. The economic activity at the port is a crucial part of the town's prosperity, and the interactions between traders, merchants, and buyers reflect the diverse and dynamic nature of the community.

Life at the Port of Dave's Landing

The port of Dave's Landing is a vital artery of the town, bustling with activity and life. Situated on the serene shores of the bay, the port is not only a hub of commerce but also a melting pot of cultures and stories. It is a place where majestic ships from distant lands dock daily, where sailors share tales of their adventures, and where the rhythmic pulse of maritime life sets the pace for the town.

The sight of majestic ships arriving and departing from the port is a daily spectacle in Dave's Landing. These vessels, each with their own unique design and history, are a testament to the town's importance as a center of trade and culture. The most common type of ships in the port are called trading vessels. These ships are built for carrying cargo across vast distances, their holds filled with goods such as spices, textiles, metals, and exotic produce. They vary in size from small, nimble schooners to large, imposing galleons. The sight of a fully laden trading ship approaching the harbor is always an exciting moment, signaling the arrival of new and diverse products to the market. The smaller, more agile fishing boats are also a common sight in the port. These vessels, often crewed by families or small teams, head out to sea early in the morning and return in the afternoon with their catch. The fishing boats are a vital part of the town's food supply, and their presence adds to the daily rhythm of port life. Merchant ships, often larger and more elaborately decorated than the average trading vessel, bring luxury goods and high-value items. These ships are a sight to behold, with their polished wood, intricate carvings, and brightly colored sails. They are typically associated with wealthy traders and carry goods such as fine silks, precious gemstones, and rare spices.

Occasionally, exploration vessels dock at the port, their crews bringing news and stories from uncharted territories. These ships are rugged and equipped for long voyages, with reinforced hulls and advanced navigation equipment. The arrival of an exploration vessel is always a significant event, sparking curiosity and excitement among the townspeople. Passenger ships, designed for comfort and speed, transport people between Dave's Landing and other ports. These vessels are equipped with cabins and amenities to ensure a pleasant journey for their passengers. The arrival and departure of passenger ships add a sense of dynamism to the port as people come and go, bringing with them new stories and experiences.

Life at the port is a whirlwind of activity, with a constant flow of people, goods, and stories. The port is a place where hard work and camaraderie go hand in hand and where the unique culture of the town is on full display. Dockworkers are the backbone of the port, responsible for loading and unloading ships, maintaining the docks, and ensuring that everything runs smoothly. These men and women are known for their strength, endurance, and teamwork. Their day begins early, often before sunrise, and continues until the last ship is secured for the night. The primary task of the dockworkers is to handle the cargo that comes in and out of the port. This involves lifting heavy crates, barrels, and sacks, often using cranes and other equipment. The work is physically demanding, but the dockworkers take pride in their efficiency and precision. Maintaining the docks and the port infrastructure is another crucial aspect of their job. This includes repairing wooden planks, reinforcing piers, and ensuring that all equipment is in working order. Regular maintenance is essential to keep the port safe and functional, and the dockworkers' expertise is highly valued.

The dockworkers form a close-knit community, relying on each other for support and assistance. Teamwork is essential, as the work often requires coordinated efforts. The camaraderie among the dockworkers is palpable, with jokes, stories, and friendly banter helping to lighten the load.

Sailors are the lifeblood of the port, bringing with them a sense of adventure and wanderlust. These men and women spend much of their lives at sea, navigating the vast oceans and braving the elements. When they dock at Dave's Landing, they bring with them not only goods but also stories and experiences from distant lands. The life of a sailor is structured yet unpredictable. When in port, sailors are busy with tasks such as repairing their ships, restocking supplies, and preparing for their next voyage. These activities require a range of skills, from carpentry and sailmaking to navigation and weather forecasting.

One of the most cherished traditions among sailors is storytelling. During their downtime, sailors gather in taverns, around bonfires, or on the decks of their ships to share tales of their adventures. These stories are a way to pass the time, bond with fellow sailors, and preserve the oral history of their journeys. The stories told by sailors often blend fact and fiction, creating a rich tapestry of legends and myths. Tales of sea monsters, ghost ships, and hidden treasures are familiar, and each sailor adds their own embellishments. These stories capture the imagination of the townspeople, keeping the spirit of adventure alive.

Music is an integral part of sailors' lives, providing both entertainment and a way to coordinate their work. Sea shanties, with their rhythmic beats and catchy lyrics, are sung as sailors haul ropes, raise sails, and perform other tasks. In the evenings, more melodic and reflective songs are sung, often accompanied by instruments such as the fiddle or accordion.

The Heart of Dave's Landing: The Marketplace

Adjacent to the docks, the marketplace is a hive of activity, where goods from the ships are displayed and sold. The marketplace of Dave's Landing is the beating heart of the town. A lively and colorful hub where the community gathers daily. From dawn till dusk, the market is a flurry of activity, with stalls and shops lining the cobblestone streets. Each vendor brings something unique to the table, contributing to the market's rich tapestry of goods and cultures.

The market stalls are filled with a dizzying array of products, from fresh fish and fruits to exotic spices and handcrafted items. Traders and merchants are the lifeblood of the marketplace. They come from various backgrounds and regions, each bringing their own unique products and trading practices. The interactions between traders are often animated, with negotiations and bartering being a common sight.

The marketplace attracts a diverse crowd of buyers, from local residents to visitors from other regions. People come to the market not only to purchase goods but also to socialize and catch up on the latest news. The lively atmosphere makes the market a focal point of community life. One of the most exciting aspects of the marketplace is the variety of exotic goods available. Spices from distant lands, rare textiles, and unique artifacts are just a few of the treasures to be found. These items not only enhance the local culture but also stimulate the economy by attracting buyers from far and wide.

In the market, people greet each other with genuine warmth. It's common to see friends and acquaintances stopping to chat, exchanging news and pleasantries. The market is not just a place for commerce but also a social hub where relationships are forged and strengthened. As you walk through the market, the first thing you notice is the diversity of people. Elves, Dwarves, Humans, and other races mingle freely, their interactions a testament to the town's inclusive ethos. The air is filled with the hum of different languages, the aromas of exotic spices, and the vibrant colors of textiles and crafts.

(Elven Artisans) Elven artisans are known for their delicate jewelry and intricate carvings. They often engage in animated conversations with customers, explaining the lore behind their creations and sharing stories from their homeland. The Elves' calm demeanor and graceful movements add a touch of elegance to the bustling market scene.

(Dwarven Smiths) Dwarven smiths, with their robust builds and hearty laughter, bring a sense of strength and reliability. Their stalls display finely crafted weapons and tools, each piece a work of art. Customers trust the Dwarves' expertise and often seek their advice on practical matters. The smiths are always ready with a story or a joke. Their camaraderie is infectious.

(Human Traders) Human traders, versatile and adaptive, offer a wide variety of goods, from fresh produce to exotic spices.

Their stalls are a riot of colors and scents, drawing in customers with their enthusiastic sales pitches. Humans are known for their knack for negotiation, and it's not uncommon to see a friendly, haggling session ending with both parties satisfied and perhaps even laughing together.

(Musical Interludes) Musicians often set up in the market, filling the air with melodies that reflect the diverse cultural heritage of Dave's Landing. A young Human plays a lute, singing ballads of heroism and love, while a group of Elves harmonize with their ethereal voices. The music creates a joyful backdrop to the market's activities, inviting people to pause and enjoy the moment.

Daily Life and Community Spirit

Life in Dave's Landing is characterized by a strong sense of community and mutual support. The town's layout, with its interconnected streets and communal spaces, encourages interaction and fosters a sense of belonging. People here value their relationships and try to maintain a harmonious environment.

In the early mornings, the town wakes up to the sound of seagulls and the gentle lapping of waves against the shore. Fishermen prepare their boats, setting out to sea with hopes of a good catch. Farmers bring fresh produce into town, their carts laden with fruits, vegetables, and flowers. Bakers open their shops, the aroma of freshly baked bread wafting through the streets.

As the sun rises, people of all ages start their day. Children head to school, their laughter and chatter echoing through the town. Schools in Dave's Landing are inclusive, teaching a curriculum that encompasses the histories, languages, and arts of all races. This approach fosters understanding and respect from a young age.

Adults go about their work, whether it's tending to shops, crafting goods, or providing services. There is a palpable sense of pride in their work, as everyone contributes to the town's prosperity. The workday is punctuated by friendly interactions, as people take time to help each other and share a kind word.

Afternoons in Dave's Landing are lively, with the marketplace at its busiest. Street performers entertain crowds with acrobatics, magic tricks, and storytelling. Food stalls offer a variety of delicacies, from Dwarven meat pies to Elven fruit tarts, catering to diverse tastes.

Workshops and studios buzz with activity as artisans and craftsmen create their wares. Apprentices from different races learn side by side, honing their skills under the guidance of experienced masters. The spirit of collaboration is strong, and it's common to see people sharing techniques and ideas, resulting in unique, hybrid creations that blend different cultural influences.

As the day winds down, the focus shifts to relaxation and socialization. Families gather for dinner, often inviting neighbors to join them. Communal meals are a common practice, reflecting the town's emphasis on togetherness. Food is shared, stories are told, and bonds are strengthened over hearty, home-cooked meals.

The town's taverns and inns come alive in the evenings, filled with laughter and music. These establishments are not just places to eat and drink but also social centers where people come to unwind and enjoy each other's company. Bards perform epic tales and lively tunes, encouraging patrons to sing along and dance. Taverns and inns play a crucial role in port life, providing sailors and visitors with food, drink, and a place to rest. These establishments are vibrant centers of social activity where stories are shared, deals are made, and friendships are forged.

The Sailor's Rest (owned by Liam's family): One of the most popular taverns in the port is The Sailor's Rest, known for its hearty meals and lively atmosphere. The tavern is a favorite gathering place for sailors, who come to relax, enjoy good food, and share stories. The walls are adorned with nautical memorabilia, and the air is filled with the sounds of laughter and music.

The Golden Anchor: The Golden Anchor is an inn that caters to traders and merchants. It offers comfortable rooms and a more refined dining experience. The inn's common room is a place where business deals are often struck, and its patrons enjoy discussing trade routes, market trends, and the latest news from distant lands.

The Mermaid's Song: A more eclectic establishment, The Mermaid's Song attracts a diverse crowd of artists, musicians, and storytellers. The inn is known for its nightly performances, where bards and musicians entertain the guests with songs and tales. The Mermaid's Song is a place of creativity and inspiration, where people from all walks of life come together to celebrate the arts.

Festivals are a vital part of life in Dave's Landing, celebrating the town's diversity and fostering a sense of unity. These events are held regularly, marking important dates and seasons. Each festival is a blend of different cultural traditions, creating a vibrant and inclusive atmosphere.

Spring Festival (Spring equinox): The Spring Festival is a celebration of renewal and growth. The town is adorned with flowers, and the air is filled with the scent of blooming plants. People wear colorful attire and participate in parades, dances, and music performances. Elves share their knowledge of herbalism, while Dwarves showcase their metalworking skills with intricate displays.

Cultural Fair (Beginning of Summer): The Cultural Fair is a celebration of the town's diversity. The Fair takes place in the town square and by the port. Each race sets up booths showcasing its traditions, crafts, and cuisines. There are performances of traditional dance music, showcases of diverse ships, ship races, and storytelling. It's an opportunity for everyone to learn about and appreciate each other's heritage, strengthening the bonds of friendship and understanding.

Harvest Festival (last days of autumn): The Harvest Festival is a time of gratitude for the bounty of the land. Farmers bring their best produce, and feasts are held in communal spaces. There are competitions for the largest vegetables, best-tasting dishes, and even friendly tug-of-war matches. Everyone contributes, and the sense of community is at its peak.

Winter Solstice: The Winter Solstice is a time of reflection and hope. The town is illuminated with lanterns and candles, creating a warm and inviting atmosphere. People exchange gifts, often handmade, and gather around bonfires to share stories and songs. It's a time to remember the past year and look forward to the future.

Festivals and celebrations are not just things of the city and of the market; they are also an integral part of life at the port. These events bring the community together, fostering a sense of unity and joy. Some of the most popular celebrations at the port are:

Port Festival: The Port Festival is a grand celebration held annually to honor the town's maritime heritage. The festival includes parades of decorated ships, sailing competitions, and performances by local musicians and dancers. The highlight of the festival is a grand feast, where people gather to enjoy a variety of dishes made from the sea's bounty.

Harvest of the Sea: The Harvest of the Sea is a celebration that is held at the end of the fishing season (towards the end of summer). Fishermen bring their best catches, and the town comes together for a day of feasting, music, and dancing. The event also includes competitions such as fish carving and boat races, adding to the festive atmosphere.

The Role of Music and Art

Music and art play a crucial role in the life of Dave's Landing. They are not just forms of entertainment but also expressions of the town's collective identity and values. Music is everywhere in Dave's Landing, from the streets and taverns to homes and communal gatherings. It reflects the town's diverse cultural heritage and serves as a unifying force.

Street performers add a lively element to the market and public spaces. They play instruments, sing, and perform acts that draw crowds and create a festive atmosphere. Their performances often include traditional songs from different cultures, celebrating the town's diversity.

In the evenings, taverns and inns are filled with music. Bards and musicians perform a mix of lively tunes and soulful ballads, encouraging patrons to join in. Singing and dancing are common, and the music fosters a sense of camaraderie and joy. During festivals, music is a central feature. Parades, dances, and performances showcase the rich musical traditions of the town's different races. The melodies and rhythms create an uplifting and inclusive atmosphere, bringing people together in celebration.

Art is another important aspect of life in Dave's Landing, reflecting the town's cultural diversity and creative spirit. The town is adorned with public art, from murals and sculptures to mosaics and carvings. These artworks often depict scenes from local legends, historical events, and everyday life, celebrating the town's heritage and values.

Artisans and craftsmen work in workshops and studios, creating a wide range of artistic products. These spaces are open to the public, allowing people to observe and learn about different techniques and styles. The collaborative environment fosters creativity and innovation, resulting in unique and beautiful creations. Regular art exhibitions are held in communal spaces, showcasing the work of local artists. These events provide a platform for artists to share their creations and for the community to appreciate and support their talent. The exhibitions often include interactive elements, such as workshops and demonstrations, encouraging people to engage with the art.

Education and Knowledge Sharing

Education is highly valued in Dave's Landing, with a strong emphasis on both academic learning and practical skills. The town's inclusive approach to education reflects its commitment to fostering understanding and cooperation among its diverse population. Schools in Dave's Landing offer a comprehensive curriculum that includes the histories, languages, and arts of all races. This holistic approach ensures that children grow up with a broad perspective and an appreciation for diversity.

Primary schools focus on foundational subjects, such as reading, writing, and mathematics, as well as the basics of different cultures and traditions. Children learn about the history and legends of their own race first at home, and they learn about everything else at school. Children attend school only to the age of 16; after that they are allowed to pursue their own interests and passions. Some take this as an opportunity to go on adventures of their own, while others take the opportunity to seek out apprenticeships or jobs in the areas that they are passionate about, like medicine, magic, or the arts. Here (at school) is where we met for the first time our protagonists (Liam, Ava, Emma, and Theo) as they are trying to explain to the main teacher why they are late for the first period.

Chapter VI:
Main Characters

Liam, with his bright blue eyes and messy brown hair, is a curious and ambitious boy, always yearning for adventure. He is the eldest of the group and is an embodiment of bravery and adventure. His courage often leads the group into thrilling escapades, exploring unknown territories and taking on challenges that others might shy away from. His leadership qualities make him a natural guide, and his adventurous spirit is contagious, inspiring his friends and family to push their boundaries and seek out new experiences. At school, Liam is known for his leadership skills and adventurous spirit. He often takes charge during group activities and is always the first to volunteer for new challenges. His classmates admire his bravery and look up to him as a role model. Liam's adventurous nature sometimes leads to him getting into trouble, but his quick thinking and resourcefulness usually help him find a way out.

His best friend, Emma, is a sharp-witted girl with a knack for solving puzzles and an adventurous spirit that matches Liam's. Emma is one of the cousins and the brains of the bunch. She is indeed the smartest of the group. Her intellect and curiosity drive her to constantly seek knowledge and solve problems. Emma's sharp mind and analytical skills often come in handy during their adventures, helping the group navigate tricky situations and uncover hidden secrets. Her love for learning and her resourcefulness make her an invaluable asset to the team. Emma's intelligence and curiosity are well-known among her classmates. She excels in her studies and is often seen helping others with their homework or explaining difficult concepts. Emma's problem-solving skills and love for learning make her a favorite among the teachers, who appreciate her dedication and enthusiasm. Her peers often turn to her for guidance and advice, valuing her intellect and insight.

Theo, a strong and loyal companion, is ever ready to protect his friends and face any challenge head-on. Theo, Emma's brother and the other cousin, is also the joker of the group. His humor and penchant for pranks keep everyone entertained, lightening the mood even in the most challenging times. Theo's playful nature and quick wit make him the life of the party, and his ability to make everyone laugh is a crucial element in maintaining the group's camaraderie and morale. At school, Theo's humor and penchant for pranks make him the class clown. He loves making his classmates laugh and is always coming up with new jokes and tricks to entertain them. Theo's playful nature sometimes gets him into trouble, but his charm and quick wit usually help him get away with it. His ability to make everyone laugh and lighten the mood is a vital part of the group's dynamic, both at school and beyond.

Ava, the gentle soul of the group, has a deep connection with nature and a calming presence that balances the group's dynamic. Ava, Liam's younger sister, is also known for her sweet demeanor and her remarkable affinity for magic. She has a natural talent for enchantments and spell-crafts, often mesmerizing her friends with her magical tricks and abilities. Ava's kindness and magical prowess make her a cherished member of the group, often bringing a touch of wonder and excitement to their daily lives. At school, this makes her very popular among her peers. She often uses her magic to entertain her friends, performing small tricks and enchantments that leave everyone in awe. Ava is also known for her kindness and willingness to help others, often going out of her way to support her classmates in need. Her gentle demeanor and magical talents make her a beloved figure at school.

The First Adventures

From a young age, the four friends are inseparable, exploring every nook and cranny of Dave's Landing. Their first adventures involve sneaking into the bustling markets or into Sailor's Rest during school hours, listening to sailors' tales of distant lands, and dreaming of the day they can embark on their own journeys. They bond over these small adventures, forming dreams of treasure hunting and exploring the unknown together.

Liam's adventurous spirit often leads the group on exciting expeditions around Sailor's Rest, a quaint inn owned by his father. Whether exploring the hidden nooks and crannies of the inn or venturing into the nearby woods, Liam's courage and leadership guide the group through thrilling escapades. His fearless nature often inspires others to push their limits and embrace new challenges. Ava's magical abilities add a touch of enchantment to their adventures at Sailor's Rest. She often uses her magic to enhance their experiences, creating illusions and enchantments that bring their stories to life and to disguise themselves from their father ("when they are up for no good," as their father would say) on their escapades. During their adventures, Emma's sharp mind and problem-solving skills come in very handy. Whether deciphering a cryptic map or figuring out how to navigate a tricky situation, Emma's intellect and resourcefulness often save the day. Her love for learning and her analytical skills make her an invaluable member of the team, helping the group overcome obstacles and uncover hidden secrets. Theo's humor and playful nature also bring a sense of fun and laughter to their adventures. He loves pulling pranks on others, keeping everyone on their toes, and ensuring that there's never a dull moment. Theo's quick wit and love for jokes make him the life of the party, and his ability to make everyone laugh is a crucial element in maintaining the group's camaraderie and morale.

Adventures by the Port

Liam's love for adventure extends to the port, where he dreams of becoming a sailor and exploring the open seas. He often leads the group on excursions to the docks, watching the ships come in and out of the bay and imagining the distant lands they might visit. Liam's courage and sense of adventure inspire others to dream big and embrace the unknown. Ava's magical abilities come to life by the port, where she often finds enchanted seashells and other magical artifacts. She loves sharing her discoveries with the group, using her magic to create enchanting experiences and bringing a sense of wonder to their seaside adventures. Emma's love for learning extends to the sea, where she studies nautical maps and learns about maritime history. Her sharp mind and curiosity drive her to uncover the secrets of the ocean, and her knowledge often comes in handy during their adventures. Theo's humor playful nature, and quick wit keep everyone entertained, and his ability to make everyone laugh is a crucial element in maintaining the group's camaraderie and morale. At the port, he loves to pull tricks on the sailors and dockworkers. His jokes and pranks add a sense of fun and laughter to their seaside adventures, ensuring that there's never a dull moment.

Helping Grandpa with the Catch of the Day

At times, the fourth of them goes out to the port to help their grandpa bring in the catch of the day. Liam's strength and courage come to the fore when helping their grandpa with the catch. He often takes on the toughest tasks, lifting heavy nets and handling the largest fish with ease. Liam's bravery and leadership make him a natural guide, and his adventurous spirit inspires others to tackle the challenges of the day with enthusiasm and determination. Ava's magical abilities prove useful when helping their grandpa. She often uses her magic to make the tasks easier, enchanting the nets to pull in more fish or using spells to clean and prepare the catch.

Emma's sharp mind and organizational skills come in handy, as she often takes charge of sorting and categorizing the fish, ensuring that everything is done efficiently and effectively. Theo's humor and playful nature bring a sense of fun and laughter to their daily chores. He loves making jokes and pulling pranks on their grandpa, keeping everyone entertained and motivated. Their interactions and adventures highlight their unique strengths and personalities. Their experiences at school, Sailor's Rest, the port, and helping their grandpa with the catch of the day bring them closer together and provide endless opportunities for growth, learning, and fun.

Chapter VII:
The Rest of the Family

Liam and Ava's Parents

Nathaniel (Nate) McAllister

Nathaniel McAllister, often called Nate, is the proud father of Liam and Ava. He owns the Sailor's Rest, a quaint inn by the port, which is well known for its hospitality and nautical charm. Nate is a former sailor who decided to settle down and create a home for his family. His deep love for the sea is reflected in the decor of the inn, which is adorned with maritime memorabilia and artifacts from his sailing days.

Nate is a tall man with a sturdy build, marked by years of labor and seafaring. His sun-tanned skin and weathered hands speak of a life spent on the open waters. Despite his tough exterior, Nate has a warm heart and a deep love for his family. He is known for his storytelling, often regaling guests and his children with tales of his adventures at sea. His courage and leadership are qualities that Liam has inherited, and he often encourages his son to be brave and adventurous.

Nate is also a loving and supportive husband to Eliza. He admires her magical abilities and often says that her enchantments brought a special kind of magic into his life. Together, they have created a loving and nurturing environment for their children, fostering their unique talents and encouraging their dreams.

Eliza McAllister (née White)

Eliza McAllister, the mother of Liam and Ava, is a gentle and kind-hearted woman with a natural talent for magic. She comes from a long line of magical practitioners and has passed on her knowledge and abilities to her daughter, Ava. Eliza's magic is subtle and enchanting, often used to create a warm and welcoming atmosphere at the Sailor's Rest.

Eliza is a petite woman with an air of grace and elegance. Her long, flowing hair and sparkling eyes give her an almost ethereal appearance. She is known for her soothing presence and her ability to calm even the most restless souls. Her magical abilities are often used to help others, whether it's healing minor injuries, finding lost items, or creating beautiful illusions to entertain guests.

Eliza is deeply connected to her children and takes great pride in their accomplishments. She nurtures Liam's adventurous spirit and encourages Ava to explore her magical talents. Her relationship with Nate is one of mutual respect and admiration, and together, they create a harmonious and loving home for their family.

Emma and Theo's Parents

Margaret (Maggie) White-Foster

Margaret Foster, known as Maggie, is the second sister of Eliza and the mother of Emma and Theo. Maggie is a vibrant and energetic woman with a sharp mind and a quick wit. She works as a librarian in the town's library, where her love for books and knowledge is evident. Maggie's intelligence and resourcefulness are traits that Emma has inherited, and she takes great pride in her daughter's academic achievements.

Maggie has a warm and inviting personality, making her a beloved figure in the community. She is always ready to lend a helping hand or offer a listening ear. Her relationship with her children is one of mutual respect and understanding. She encourages Emma's love for learning and supports Theo's playful nature, understanding that humor is an important part of their family dynamic.

Maggie's relationship with her husband, Daniel, is one of partnership and support. They complement each other perfectly, with Maggie's intelligence and Daniel's creativity making them a formidable team. Together, they create a nurturing and stimulating environment for their children, encouraging them to explore their interests and develop their unique talents.

Daniel Foster

Daniel Foster, the father of Emma and Theo, is a talented artist and musician. He works as an art teacher at the local school and is known for his creativity and passion for the arts. Daniel's artistic talents have been passed down to his children, especially Theo, who shares his father's love for music and creativity.

Daniel is a tall, lean man with an easygoing demeanor. His long hair and casual attire give him a bohemian appearance, and his infectious enthusiasm for the arts makes him a favorite among his students. He is known for his imaginative teaching methods and his ability to inspire creativity in others.

Daniel's relationship with Maggie is one of mutual admiration and respect. They support each other's passions and work together to create a loving and stimulating environment for their children. Daniel's playful nature and love for pranks are traits that Theo has inherited, and they often bond over their shared sense of humor.

The Single Uncle

Uncle Jack White

Jack White, the younger brother of Eliza and Maggie, is a sailor in charge of a merchant ship. Uncle Jack is a rugged and adventurous man known for his daring exploits and love for the sea. He often regales his nieces and nephews with tales of his voyages, inspiring Liam's dreams of becoming a sailor.

Uncle Jack is a tall, muscular man with a commanding presence. His weathered face and piercing eyes reflect a life of adventure and excitement. Despite his tough exterior, Jack has a soft spot for his family, especially his nieces and nephews. He enjoys spending time with them, sharing his knowledge of the sea, and teaching them about the world beyond their small town.

Jack's relationship with his sisters is one of deep affection and respect. He admires Eliza's magical abilities and Maggie's intelligence, and he often seeks their advice and support. His bond with Nate is also strong, as they share a mutual love for the sea and a deep respect for each other's experiences.

Uncle Jack's presence in the family adds an element of excitement and adventure, and his stories of the sea captivate the imaginations of Liam, Ava, Emma, and Theo. He serves as a role model for Liam, encouraging him to embrace his adventurous spirit and pursue his dreams.

Grandpa

Grandpa Robert White

Grandpa Robert, the father of Eliza, Maggie, and Jack, is a retired fisherman with a wealth of knowledge about the sea. Grandpa Robert is a beloved figure in the family, known for his wisdom, kindness, and gentle nature. He often shares his stories and experiences with his grandchildren, teaching them valuable life lessons and passing on his love for the sea.

Grandpa Robert is a tall, sturdy man with a kind face and a twinkle in his eye. His white hair and beard give him a distinguished appearance, and his gentle demeanor makes him a comforting presence. Despite his age, Grandpa Robert is still active and enjoys helping the Inn with (his) catch of the day, something that he also uses to pass on his skills and knowledge to his grandchildren (when they help).

Grandpa Robert's relationship with his family is one of deep love and respect. He is a source of wisdom and guidance for his children and grandchildren, always ready to offer advice and support. His bond with Liam is particularly strong, as they share a mutual love for adventure and the sea. Grandpa Robert's stories and teachings have a profound impact on his grandchildren, shaping their values and inspiring their dreams.

Conclusion

The McAllister and White-Foster families are a close-knit and loving group, united by their shared experiences and mutual support. Their interactions are characterized by mutual respect, support, and affection, creating a warm and nurturing environment for the children. Nate and Eliza's nurturing home, Maggie and Daniel's stimulating environment, Uncle Jack's adventurous spirit, and Grandpa Robert's wisdom create a dynamic and engaging family life.

Liam, Ava, Emma, and Theo thrive in this supportive environment, developing their unique talents and forming lasting bonds with each other and their extended family. The family also faces challenges together, supporting each other through difficult times and learning valuable lessons. Whether it's dealing with a crisis at the Sailor's Rest, navigating personal struggles, or overcoming obstacles during their adventures, the family's unity and resilience help them persevere and grow stronger. These challenges provide opportunities for the children to develop their skills and character, guided by the wisdom and support of their parents and grandparents. The family's strength and love create a nurturing environment where each member can thrive and achieve their potential. Their interactions and adventures highlight the importance of family, love, and support, creating a foundation for their growth and happiness. The family's stories and experiences inspire and guide the children, shaping their values and dreams and preparing them for the future.

Part II:

The adventure begins.
Maeve and the introduction to the legend of the
Sea Train.

Chapter VIII:
The Woods, The Entrance to The Jungle, and The Voice of a Lost Civilization

As they grow older, their adventures take them further into the outskirts of the city. They discover hidden groves, abandoned buildings, and mysterious artifacts that fuel their imaginations. Each friend develops unique skills: Emma becomes adept at deciphering ancient maps, Theo hones his physical strength and bravery, Ava deepens her understanding of nature, magic, and wildlife, and Liam, the natural leader, learns to navigate and plan their expeditions.

Their friendship strengthens as they face and overcome various challenges together. They encounter minor threats, such as wild animals or unfriendly strangers, but their unity and resourcefulness always see them through. Away from the natural protection of the city, they turn to face their first major challenge as they venture into the mysteries that Aeloria has claimed for its own.

Into The Woods:

The sun hung high in the sky, casting dappled shadows through the dense canopy of the forest. It was a perfect summer day, with a gentle breeze rustling the leaves and the scent of pine and earth filling the air. Liam, Ava, Emma, and Theo had gathered at the edge of the woods, excitement buzzing between them like an electric current.

Liam, now fifteen and the eldest of the group, led the way. His once boyish features had started to sharpen, hinting at the man he would soon become. He carried a well-worn leader pack filled with supplies, and his confident stride suggested he had spent many hours planning this adventure. Ava, thirteen and always the curious one, followed close behind. Her dark hair, usually tied back in a neat ponytail, had come loose, and she absentmindedly tucked stray strands behind her ear. Her bright eyes scanned the surroundings, taking in every detail. She carried a notebook and a pencil, ready to document any discoveries they might make. Emma, at fourteen, walked beside her. She was the quietest of the group, preferring to observe and listen rather than lead. Her long, auburn hair was braided neatly, and her thoughtful expression hinted at the stories she was already crafting in her mind about their upcoming adventure. She carried a compass that grandpa had given her two winters ago around her neck, eager to uncover history and hidden secrets. Theo, the youngest at twelve, brought up the rear. His boundless energy was evident in the way he practically bounced with every step. His leader pack was almost as large as he was, packed to the brim with snacks, gadgets, and anything he thought might come in handy. He was the most excited about the adventure and what they may find, imagining all sorts of hidden treasures and secrets waiting to be uncovered. He was also making fun of Liam, as he was very serious about the day and being quiet.

The woods closest to their city were familiar territory, a place they had explored countless times during their childhood. But today, they were venturing deeper, following a path that had always intrigued them but had never been fully explored. As they walked, the sounds of the city faded away, replaced by the chirping of birds and the rustle of small animals in the underbrush.

"I can't believe we're finally doing this," Theo said, his voice brimming with excitement. "We've talked about it for so long!"

"Yeah," Liam replied, glancing back with a smile. "It's about time we had another adventure. We've all been so busy with school and everything."

Ava nodded. "I wonder what we'll find. The stories about the ruins are so old, and no one really knows what's out there."

"That's what makes it exciting," Emma added, her voice soft but filled with anticipation. "It's like stepping into a mystery."

They continued along the path, the undergrowth growing thicker as they ventured further from the city. The trail, once clear and well-trodden, became narrower and more overgrown. They had to push through bushes and duck under low-hanging branches, but their determination never wavered.

After what felt like hours, they emerged into a small clearing. The sunlight broke through the canopy, illuminating the ancient stones scattered across the ground. The ruins, partially hidden by creeping vines and moss, stood like silent sentinels at the edge of the jungle.

"Wow," Ava breathed, taking in the sight. "It's even more incredible than I imagined."

Liam walked forward, his eyes scanning the area. "Let's set up a base camp here," he suggested. "We can explore the ruins and see what we find. We'll need to be careful, though. The jungle can be dangerous."

They set to work, their movements synchronized from years of adventuring together. Liam and Theo pitched a tent and organized their supplies while Ava and Emma examined the ruins more closely. The stones were weathered and covered in carvings, symbols that hinted at a long-forgotten civilization.

"These carvings are fascinating," Ava said, running her fingers over the intricate patterns. "I wish we knew what they meant."

"Maybe we can figure it out," Emma replied, making some sketches of them. "Or find someone who can help us translate them."

As the day turned to evening, they gathered around a small campfire, sharing stories and theories about the ruins. The jungle seemed to come alive at night, the sounds of nocturnal creatures creating a symphony around them.

"We should take turns keeping watch," Liam suggested. "Just in case. I'll take the first shift."

The others nodded, and soon, Theo, Ava, and Emma were asleep in the tent, leaving Liam alone by the fire. He stared into the flames, his mind racing with possibilities. What secrets did the jungle hold? What stories were etched into the ancient stones?

His thoughts were interrupted by a rustling in the bushes. He tensed, his hand instinctively reaching for the light beside him. The noise grew louder, and he stood, ready to investigate.

"Liam?" A voice whispered.

He turned to see Ava, her eyes wide with curiosity. "I couldn't sleep," she admitted. "Can I keep you company?"

Liam nodded, relieved to have someone to share the watch with. They sat in silence for a while, listening to the sounds of the jungle.

"Do you think we'll find anything important?" Ava asked eventually.

"I don't know," Liam replied honestly. "But whatever we find, we'll face it together."

The Ruins:

The night passed uneventfully, and by morning, they were all eager to begin their exploration. They decided to split into pairs, covering more ground that way. Liam and Ava took one side of the ruins while Emma and Theo explored the other.

Liam and Ava moved carefully, examining each stone and carving. The deeper they went, the more complex the symbols became, almost as if they were telling a story. Ava sketched them in her notebook, hoping to piece together their meaning later.

Meanwhile, Emma and Theo discovered what looked like the entrance to an underground chamber. The opening was small and partially covered by debris, but it was clear that it led somewhere important.

"Should we go in?" Theo asked, his voice trembling with excitement.

Emma hesitated. "Let's get Liam and Ava first. We shouldn't go in alone."

They hurried back to the clearing, calling for their friends. Liam and Ava arrived quickly, and together, they returned to the entrance.

"This is it," Liam said, peering into the darkness. "Whatever's down there, it's been hidden for a long time."

With torches in hand, they carefully made their way inside. The air was cool and damp, and the walls were lined with more carvings. The tunnel sloped downward, leading them deeper into the earth.

After what felt like an eternity, they emerged into a large chamber. The room was filled with ancient artifacts, pottery, and tools, all covered in a thick layer of dust. In the center of the room stood a pedestal, and on it rested a small, ornate box.

"Look at this," Ava said, her voice barely above a whisper. "It must be important."

Liam approached the pedestal cautiously. "It looks like a puzzle box," he said, examining it closely. "I think we can open it, but we need to be careful."

They gathered around, each taking a turn to study the box. The carvings on its surface were similar to the ones they had seen outside, and it became clear that the symbols were the key to opening it.

It took hours of careful work, but finally, the box clicked open. Inside, they found a set of scrolls, their edges brittle with age.

"These must be ancient writings," Emma said, her eyes wide with awe. "We need to get these back to camp and see if we can decipher them."

They returned to their camp, their discovery fueling their excitement. As the sun set, they pored over the scrolls, trying to make sense of the faded text.

"It looks like a map," Ava said, pointing to a series of drawings. "But I can't tell where it leads."

"Maybe it's a treasure map," Theo suggested. "Or a guide to something even more important."

Liam nodded. "Whatever it is, it's part of our adventure now. We'll figure it out together."

The days that followed were filled with exploration and discovery. They ventured deeper into the jungle, following the clues from the scrolls. Each step brought them closer to unraveling the mystery of the ruins and the civilization that had once thrived there.

Their bond grew stronger with each challenge they faced, and their teamwork and trust in one another were unwavering. They knew that whatever lay ahead, they would face it together, just as they always had.

As they stood at the edge of a vast, hidden valley, the sun rising behind them, they felt a sense of accomplishment and anticipation. Their second adventure had only just begun, and the possibilities were endless.

"Ready?" Liam asked, his voice steady and confident.

"Ready," Ava, Emma, and Theo replied in unison.

With that, they stepped forward into the jungle to head back home, their hearts filled with the promise of discovery and the thrill of adventure, and their minds filled with questions about what all those symbols meant and what treasures they would uncover along the way.

Chapter IX:
The Return Home and the Task of Unraveling the Mystery of the Scroll

Liam, Ava, Emma, and Theo trudged along the dusty road, the weight of their recent adventure hanging heavily on their shoulders. The ruins had been a labyrinth of forgotten corridors and ancient secrets, culminating in the discovery of a scroll that now lay securely in Liam's satchel. They had set out in search of history, but what they found was a mystery that would follow them for years to come.

The village came into view as the sun dipped below the horizon, casting a warm, golden glow over the familiar landscape. It was a welcome sight after the eerie silence of the ruins, a reminder that they were finally home. As they approached the village gates, they were greeted by a chorus of familiar voices, friends, and family rushing to meet them.

"Liam, Ava, Emma, Theo! You're back!" Mrs. Harper, the village baker, exclaimed, her flour-dusted hands clapping together in joy. "We were beginning to worry."

"We're fine, Mrs. Harper," Ava assured her, smiling despite her exhaustion. "Just tired and hungry."

Over the next few days, life returned to normal—or as normal as it could with the scroll constantly on their minds. Two years since their fateful adventure into the ruins, Liam, Ava, Emma, and Theo had each grown and changed in ways they hadn't anticipated. The discovery of the mysterious scroll had not only altered the course of their lives but had also deepened their bonds and honed their individual strengths. The scroll itself was a source of endless fascination and frustration. Its symbols seemed to defy all attempts at deciphering, each new theory leading to more questions than answers. Yet, it was this very mystery that kept the group going, a tantalizing enigma that promised untold secrets and unimaginable discoveries.

The fourth of them had always been intellectual and passionate about learning, but the scroll had ignited a new level of scholarly passion within them all. They had spent countless hours in the city's library, pouring over ancient texts and learning about obscure languages and forgotten civilizations. Liam's room had transformed into a labyrinth of books, scrolls, and notes, each page filled with their meticulous handwriting and ideas of what the scroll my talk about. The frustration of not being able to decipher the scroll had been a double-edged sword for the group. On one hand, it has driven them to new heights of academic excellence; on the other, it has haunted their every waking moment. They often found Themselves lost in thought, replaying their adventure in the ruins and wondering what vital clue they might have missed.

Yet, despite the setbacks, the group's excitement never waned. Every new piece of information, no matter how small, felt like a step closer to unraveling the mystery. The challenge of the scroll also fostered a new level of patience and perseverance in them. They had learned to embrace the process of trial and error, understanding that each failure brought them one step closer to success.

The scroll had become a part of their lives, a constant presence that influenced their thoughts and actions. It was a reminder of their shared adventure, a symbol of the bond they had forged in the ruins. Despite the setbacks and frustrations, it filled them with a sense of excitement and purpose, a feeling that they were on the brink of something extraordinary. When it came to deciphering the scroll, each of them had taken a separate approach and focused on how to best understand its mystery and solution. For Liam, it has been more about maps and keeping everyone on task. For Ava, it was languages, so the scroll had pushed her to explore linguistic frontiers she hadn't even known existed. She had taught herself several ancient languages, from forgotten dialects to runic scripts, hoping to find a match for the symbols on the scroll. Emma had always been practical and grounded, but the adventure had sparked a newfound interest in history and archaeology. She had taken to studying ancient civilizations, not just for the sake of the scroll but out of genuine curiosity. Her home had become a mini-museum of artifacts and historical texts, each item a piece of the puzzle she was trying to solve. The scroll had taught Emma the importance of context. She had learned to look beyond the symbols and consider the culture, beliefs, and practices of the people who might have created it. This holistic approach not only broadened her understanding of history but also deepened her appreciation for the complexities of the past. Emma's excitement was a quiet, steady flame. She found joy in the meticulous process of piecing together historical clues, knowing that each discovery brought them closer to understanding the scroll. For Theo, the scroll had given him a new purpose, driving him to explore not just the physical world and make jokes to light up the mood but also the intellectual one. He had become a master of research, uncovering obscure references and forgotten legends that might hold the key to the scroll's secrets. The challenge of the scroll also taught Theo the value of patience and discipline. He had learned to balance his impulsive nature with a more methodical approach, understanding that the answers they sought would not come easily and that not everything is about having fun and playing tricks on others. Theo's excitement was palpable. Every clue, every new theory, was a potential breakthrough. He thrived on the sense of adventure the scroll provided, knowing that their journey was far from over.

Each member of the group had their own relationship with the scroll, their own theories and approaches. But it was their combined efforts, their unique strengths and perspectives, that brought them closer to the truth. They had learned to rely on each other, to value each other's contributions, and to work together as a cohesive unit. As the months turned into years, the group never lost hope. They knew that the answers they sought were out there, waiting to be discovered. And with each passing day, they grew more determined to uncover the secrets of the scroll and to unlock the mysteries of the ancient civilization that had created it. The scroll was more than just an artifact; it was a journey, a challenge, and a promise of adventure. And for Liam, Ava, Emma, and Theo, it was a journey they were determined to see through to the end.

Chapter X:
The Mysterious Woman

By the third year, after their return, the group's frustration reached its peak. They had tried everything they could think of, consulting with scholars, experimenting with different decoding techniques, and even seeking out rumored experts in forgotten languages. But nothing worked. The symbols remained as inscrutable as the day they found the scroll.

Liam sat at his desk, surrounded by stacks of books and papers, rubbing his temples in frustration. "There has to be something we're missing," he muttered to himself. "Some clue we've overlooked."

Ava, sitting across from him, sighed heavily. "We've been over this a hundred times, Liam. Maybe it's just... undecipherable."

Emma and Theo entered the room, carrying a tray of tea and biscuits. "Any luck?" Theo asked, though he already knew the answer.

"None," Liam replied, leaning back in his chair. "I'm starting to think Ava might be right. Maybe we're chasing a ghost."

Emma placed a reassuring hand on his shoulder. "Don't say that. We'll figure it out. We just need a fresh perspective."

That fresh perspective came one sunny afternoon when the group decided to take a break from their studies and visit the local market. It was a bustling place, filled with vendors selling everything from fresh produce to handmade crafts. It was also a welcome distraction from the endless cycle of questions and dead ends.

As they wandered through the market, Emma noticed a narrow alleyway they had never explored before. "Hey, look at this," she said, pointing. "Want to see where it leads?"

The others agreed, eager for a change of scenery. The alleyway wound through the backstreets of the market, eventually leading to a small, unassuming shop tucked away in a corner. The sign above the door read "Maeve's Curiosities."

Intrigued, they entered the shop, a bell above the door chiming softly. Inside, the air was thick with the scent of incense, and the shelves were lined with an eclectic mix of items: old books, strange artifacts, and curious trinkets. Behind the counter stood a woman with long, silver hair and piercing blue eyes. She greeted them with a gentle smile.

"Welcome to my shop," she said in a voice that was both soothing and mysterious. "I'm Maeve. How can I help you today?"

Chapter XI:
Maeve's Mystique

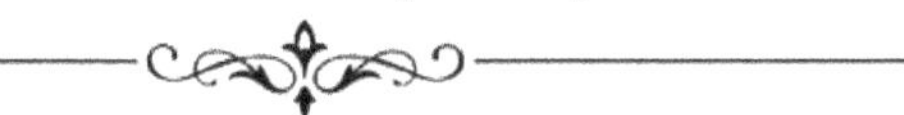

Maeve's presence was almost otherworldly. She moved with grace, her face lined with age but her eyes sharp and knowing that suggested she was no stranger to secrets and mysteries. Her eyes seemed to see right through them as if she already knew why they were there.

"We're… looking for help," Theo began, glancing at the others. "With something we can't figure out."

Maeve's smile widened slightly. "You've come to the right place. I have a knack for solving puzzles. What seems to be the problem?"

Liam reached into his satchel and carefully pulled out the scroll. "We found this two years ago in the ruins outside our village. We've been trying to decipher it ever since, but nothing seems to work."

Maeve took the scroll and unrolled it on the counter, her eyes scanning the symbols. For a moment, she said nothing, her expression thoughtful. Then, she looked up at them, her eyes gleaming with curiosity. "This is quite fascinating. These symbols are unlike anything I've seen before, but they do bear some resemblance to ancient runic languages."

The group watched in awe as Maeve began to work. She pulled out a series of old, weathered books from a nearby shelf and cross-referenced the symbols with the texts. Her movements were deliberate, almost ritualistic, as if she was performing a sacred task. Hours passed, but none of them minded. There was a sense of progress in the air, a feeling that they were finally on the verge of a breakthrough.

As the day turned into night, Maeve looked up from the scroll, her face illuminated by the soft glow of a nearby lantern. "I think I've found something," she said, her voice tinged with excitement. "These symbols… they form a map. And not just any map. It's a map to a hidden treasure, one that's been lost for centuries."

The group exchanged incredulous looks. A hidden treasure? It seemed almost too good to be true. But Maeve's conviction was undeniable. She continued to decipher the symbols, explaining their meaning and significance as she went along. It was as if the scroll was finally revealing its secrets, one symbol at a time.

By the time Maeve finished, the group was buzzing with excitement. They had a new purpose, a new adventure to embark on. And this time, they had Maeve to guide them.

With the scroll's secrets unveiled, the group felt a renewed sense of determination. Maeve had not only deciphered the symbols but had also provided them with a wealth of knowledge about the ancient civilization that had created the map. It was a civilization shrouded in mystery, known for its advanced knowledge and hidden treasures.

"Thank you, Maeve," Liam said, his voice filled with gratitude. "We couldn't have done this without you."

Maeve smiled, her eyes twinkling. "It was my pleasure. But remember, the path to the treasure won't be easy. There will be challenges along the way. You must be prepared for anything."

The group nodded, their minds already racing with plans and preparations. They knew the journey ahead would be difficult, but they were ready to face whatever came their way. With Maeve's guidance and the knowledge they had gained, they felt confident that they could uncover the hidden treasure and unlock the secrets of the ancient civilization.

As they left Maeve's shop, the group felt a sense of camaraderie and purpose that they hadn't felt in years. The scroll had brought them together, and now it was leading them on a new adventure, one that promised to be even more thrilling and dangerous than the last.

Maeve rushes out as they leave and meets with them on the street. She tells them that there's one more thing that she needs to tell them about the treasure. "Would you guys come back to see me sometime later" "I would like to tell you guys over tea." They all nodded and continued their travel home.

And so, with hearts full of hope and determination, Liam, Ava, Emma, and Theo set out once more, ready to face whatever challenges lay ahead and uncover the secrets of the past.

Chapter XII:
Maeve's introduction: The Sea Train

Several days had passed since Liam, Ava, Emma, and Theo had first visited Maeve's shop. Their minds buzzed with the revelations she had shared, and the promise of a new adventure kept them in a state of eager anticipation. Today, they were returning to Maeve's shop, their hearts a mix of excitement and nervousness. The possibility of uncovering more about the scroll and their next steps was tantalizing.

As they approached the unassuming door of Maeve's Curiosities, they could hear the faint tinkle of the shop's bell. The scent of incense wafted out, a blend of lavender and something more exotic. Maeve was behind the counter, working on a potion that shimmered with an iridescent glow. She looked up and smiled warmly as they entered.

"Welcome back, my friends," she said, her voice a soothing balm. "Please, come in and sit by the fire."

They followed her gesture to the cozy seating area, where a crackling fire cast a warm glow. Maeve moved gracefully to the hearth, where she set a kettle over the flames to boil. She joined them, her expression one of calm anticipation.

"So, you are ready to learn about the Sea Train," Maeve began, her eyes twinkling with a mix of mystery and knowledge. "It is a tale steeped in legend and adventure, much like your own journey."

The group leaned in, captivated by the allure of Maeve's storytelling. She began to speak, her voice weaving the tale with an almost magical cadence.

Maeve spoke of the Sea Train, a legendary vessel said to ride the ocean waves and the clouds alike. It was a ship of wonders, capable of traveling anywhere in the world within hours. According to legend, the Sea Train was hidden somewhere on Aeloria, and only those pure of heart and strong of spirit could find it.

"The scroll will lead you guys to it, but the journey will not be easy."

The Legend of the Sea Train

"Many centuries ago," Maeve started, "in a time when the world was still young and full of wonders, there existed a magnificent marvel known as the Sea Train. It was not a train in the conventional sense but a wondrous vessel that could traverse both land and sea, bridging the realms of the known world with the mysterious depths of the ocean.

"The Sea Train was built by an ancient civilization, one that possessed knowledge far beyond our current understanding. They were the same people who created the map you found on the scroll. Their city, hidden beneath the waves, was said to be a place of unimaginable beauty and technological prowess.

"The Sea Train was their greatest achievement. It was powered by a rare and powerful crystal known as the Heart of the Ocean. This crystal not only fueled the Sea Train but also held the key to the civilization's prosperity. The train could travel great distances in a fraction of the time it would take by any other means, connecting distant lands and bringing peace and prosperity to all it touched.

"But, as with many great things, envy and greed eventually led to the civilization's downfall. A rival faction sought to claim the Heart of the Ocean for themselves. In a final act of desperation, the guardians of the Sea Train hid it away, ensuring it would not fall into the wrong hands. The train, along with the Heart of the Ocean, was lost to time, its location a closely guarded secret known only to a few.

"The map you discovered is one of the few remaining clues to its whereabouts. It speaks of a journey fraught with peril but also of great rewards for those brave enough to seek it."

Maeve paused, allowing the weight of her words to sink in. The group sat in silence, their minds racing with possibilities. The idea of discovering the Sea Train and the Heart of the Ocean was beyond anything they had imagined.

"The journey ahead," Maeve continued, "will not be easy. The path to the Sea Train is filled with challenges, both physical and mental. You will face tests of courage, intelligence, and perseverance. But I believe you are up to the task."

Liam, ever the adventurer, leaned forward. "What do we need to do? How do we begin?"

Maeve smiled, sensing their readiness. "Your first task is to locate the entrance to the underwater city. According to the scroll, it lies somewhere along the coast, hidden by powerful enchantments. You must find the markers left by the ancient guardians, symbols that will guide you to the hidden passage."

Emma nodded, her practical mind already considering the logistics. "What kind of markers should we look for?"

"Look for symbols similar to those on the scroll," Maeve explained. "They will be carved into stones or hidden within natural formations. The guardians were masters of blending their signs with the environment." Maeve emphasized: "Maybe deeper into the jungle you can find them, and with them other pieces to the puzzle."

Theo couldn't hide his excitement. "And once we find the entrance?"

Maeve's expression grew serious. "Once you find the entrance, you will need to navigate through the submerged tunnels. There will be traps and puzzles designed to protect the city from intruders. The Heart of the Ocean will be at the center of the city, likely guarded by formidable defenses." "Maybe you guys would be blessed by the Gods and find help along the way."

Ava spoke up. "Will we need to decipher more of the ancient language?"

"Yes," Maeve confirmed. "Understanding the language will be crucial. The guardians left behind many inscriptions that will help you navigate and survive the trials ahead."

The group exchanged determined glances. They had faced many challenges together, and this new quest, though daunting, was an opportunity they couldn't pass up.

Maeve stood, her presence commanding yet gentle. "I have something for you," she said, walking over to a wooden chest in the corner of the room. She opened it and retrieved a small, intricately carved box. "This contains a vial of the same potion I was working on when you arrived. It will help you breathe underwater for a limited time. When the time comes, use it wisely."

She handed the box to Liam, who accepted it with a mixture of reverence and gratitude. "Thank you, Maeve. We won't let you down."

Maeve smiled warmly. "I know you won't. Remember, the Sea Train is not just a treasure. It's a symbol of the ancient civilization's hope and ingenuity. Treat it with the respect it deserves."

As they prepared to leave, Maeve gave them one final piece of advice. "Trust in each other and in your abilities. The path ahead is treacherous, but I believe in you. Now go, and may your journey be as enlightening as it is rewarding."

With hearts full of excitement and a renewed sense of purpose, Liam, Ava, Emma, and Theo left Maeve's shop. The legend of the Sea Train and the promise of uncovering its secrets filled them with determination. They knew the journey would be fraught with challenges, but together, they were ready to face whatever lay ahead.

As they walked through the bustling market and out into the open road, they felt the weight of their new adventure settling on their shoulders. But it was a weight they carried gladly, driven by the thrill of discovery and the bonds of friendship that had grown stronger with each passing day.

Their journey to find the Sea Train and the Heart of the Ocean had begun. And with Maeve's wisdom and their combined strengths, they were ready to face the mysteries and dangers that awaited them beneath the waves.

Part III:

In search of the Sea Train

Chapter XIII:
The Preparations

Maeve's story planted a seed of curiosity in Liam's heart. He spent his days helping his father with fishing and his evenings in the market, listening to Maeve's stories. She told him of ancient maps, mystical beasts guarding hidden paths, and the courage needed to embark on such a quest.

Liam's friends, Emma and Theo, were just as fascinated. Together, they made a pact to find the Sea Train and explore the world beyond Aeloria. They spent countless hours discussing their plans, pouring over old books, and mapping out possible routes.

With their eyes set on a grand adventure, they begin preparing in earnest. They gather resources, study maps, and learn about the wider world beyond Dave's Landing. Their dreams become more concrete as they plan a treasure-seeking expedition.

However, the teenage years are not without conflicts. Differences in opinions and personalities sometimes lead to arguments, but these are always resolved, strengthening their bond. They face external threats, too, from natural disasters to rival treasure hunters, but each challenge only solidifies their determination and unity. With the map in their possession, Liam and his friends began their journey. The first symbols led them deep into the jungle; the scroll, now partially deciphered with Maeve's help, guided them through the dense foliage and towards a forgotten part of the jungle where other ancient ruins lay hidden. Their trek was arduous, filled with the sounds of unknown creatures and the oppressive humidity of the jungle. The air was thick with the scent of damp earth and exotic flowers. Each step was a reminder of the challenges they had already faced and the ones yet to come.

The Encounter with the Drakkenbeast

As they pushed deeper into the jungle, the ruins began to appear, their ancient stone structures entwined with thick vines and moss. These ruins were different from the ones they had explored before—grander, more ominous. The air around them seemed to buzz with an ancient energy, a testament to the civilization that had once thrived here.

It was in this setting that they encountered the Drakkenbeast.

The Drakkenbeast was a massive creature, part dragon and part serpent, with scales that shimmered like molten metal in the dappled sunlight filtering through the jungle canopy. Its eyes glowed with an eerie intelligence, and its breath was a noxious mix of smoke and fire.

The beast emerged from the shadows of the ruins, its roar echoing through the jungle and sending birds and smaller creatures scattering. Liam, Ava, Emma, and Theo stood their ground, drawing their weapons and readying themselves for a battle they knew would be fierce.

Theo, always the bravest of them all, was the first to strike. He leaped forward with his sword, aiming for the Drakkenbeast's vulnerable underbelly. The beast was quick, however, and it swatted him away with a powerful tail swipe. Theo landed hard; the wind knocked out of him, but his spirit remained unbroken.

Ava began to chant an incantation she had learned from one of Maeve's books. Her voice rose above the chaos, and a shimmering barrier of light formed around her friends, deflecting the beast's fiery breath.

Emma, with a newfound appreciation for ancient combat techniques, used her knowledge to exploit the creature's weaknesses. She directed the group, calling out to Liam to aim for the beast's eyes and instructing Theo to strike its legs.

Liam had brought a bow and a quiver of arrows tipped with a special concoction Maeve had given them. He took careful aim and let loose an arrow that struck the Drakkenbeast in the eye, causing it to roar in pain and fury.

The battle raged on, the group working in perfect harmony, their movements synchronized as they combined their strengths and knowledge. Finally, with a well-placed strike from Theo's sword and a final incantation from Ava, the Drakkenbeast let out a final, deafening roar before collapsing in defeat.

The Temple at the Center of the Ruins

Panting and bruised but victorious, the group stood over the fallen beast, catching their breath and tending to their wounds. The thrill of victory was tempered by the realization that their journey was far from over. The ruins still held secrets, and they were determined to uncover them.

At the center of the ruins stood a grand temple, its stone steps worn with age but still imposing. The entrance was flanked by statues of ancient warriors, their expressions stern and watchful. The temple seemed to call to them, its interior shrouded in darkness and mystery.

As they entered the temple, the air grew cooler, and the sounds of the jungle faded away, replaced by an eerie silence. The walls were adorned with intricate carvings and murals, telling the story of the ancient civilization and their legendary Sea Train.

Deeper into the temple, they ventured, guided by the faint glow of their torches. It was in the innermost chamber that they found the piece of stone adornment. It lay on a pedestal, partially covered in dust and grime, but its golden and silver lines glinted in the torchlight, revealing its true beauty.

Emma stepped forward, carefully examining the artifact. "This looks like it's part of something larger," she said, her voice echoing in the chamber. "We need to find the rest of it."

Ava nodded, her eyes scanning the room for clues. "Look at these murals," she said, pointing to the walls. "They depict a journey—a quest for the Heart of the Ocean. I think this piece is a key, a part of a map or a puzzle that will lead us to the Sea Train."

Liam and Theo joined them, their excitement growing. "We need to find the other pieces," Liam said, his scholarly mind already piecing together the possibilities. "If we can complete the adornment, it will guide us to the Heart of the Ocean."

They spent hours in the chamber, carefully examining every detail and noting down anything that might be useful. The carvings on the walls depicted various trials and challenges, each one representing a piece of the puzzle they needed to solve.

A New Path Forward

With the piece of stone adornment safely in their possession (Ava made it into a necklace), the group made their way out of the temple, their minds buzzing with the possibilities that lay ahead. They had a new goal: to find the remaining pieces of the adornment and unlock the secrets of the Sea Train.

As they emerged from the temple, a new symbol on an opposite wall matched one of the other symbols on the scroll and talked about a place somewhere in the jungle where rivers meet.

At the entrance of the temple, the jungle greeted them with its cacophony of sounds and vibrant colors. The path ahead was uncertain and fraught with danger, but their resolve was stronger than ever. They knew that each step they took brought them closer to uncovering the secrets of the ancient civilization and the legendary Sea Train.

Theo, ever the optimist, turned to his friends with a grin. "Well, that was fun. Ready for the next part of the adventure?"

Ava laughed, her spirits lifted by their victory and the promise of what lay ahead. "Always. Let's find the rest of the pieces and see where this journey takes us."

Emma and Liam nodded in agreement; their determination was reflected in their eyes. They were a team, bound by friendship and a shared purpose. Together, they could face any challenge and uncover any mystery.

As they set off into the jungle once more, the sun began to set, casting a golden glow over the ruins and the path ahead. The journey was long, and the dangers were many, but the promise of discovery and the thrill of adventure filled their hearts with excitement.

And so, with the piece of stone adornment in hand and the legend of the Sea Train guiding their way, Liam, Ava, Emma, and Theo continued their quest, ready to face whatever challenges lay ahead and unlock the secrets of the ancient past.

Chapter XIV:
The Second Leg of The Journey

After two days of rest and resupplying their packs in the safety of a small village at the jungle's edge, Liam, Ava, Emma, and Theo set out once more. With the map in their possession, Liam and his friends began their journey. The first challenge was to decipher the symbols, which led them deep into the jungle. Their destination was a place spoken of in the ancient texts of the scroll: where the rivers kiss. The path was treacherous, lined with dangerous plants that oozed toxic sap and teemed with animals both fierce and elusive.

The jungle grew denser as they progressed, the thick canopy above filtering sunlight into a soft, green glow. The air was humid and heavy, carrying the scent of damp earth and wildflowers. Insects buzzed around them, and the occasional call of exotic birds pierced the steady hum of the jungle. As they journeyed, Liam grew more determined. The legend of the Sea Train was no longer just a story; it was a calling. He felt a sense of purpose and adventure, unlike anything he had known before. The mysteries of Aeloria, the wisdom of Maeve, and the support of his friends fueled his spirit as they ventured deeper into the unknown, inching closer to the legendary Sea Train.

The Cascades

After hours of trudging through the dense underbrush, they arrived at a set of cascades. Water tumbled down a series of rocky ledges, creating a symphony of splashes and murmurs. From the top of the cascades, they could see their next destination: a large, flat clearing surrounded by ancient stone structures, almost hidden by the encroaching jungle.

"This must be it," Emma said, her eyes wide with wonder. "The place where the rivers kiss."

Liam nodded, studying the view. "We need to find a safe way down these cascades. The scroll mentioned that our path lies beyond this point."

They began their descent, carefully picking their way down the slippery rocks. The cascades were beautiful but perilous, the stones slick with moss and the water rushing swiftly around their feet. They moved slowly, ensuring each step was secure before continuing.

Encounter with the Shadow Panther

Halfway down, Theo, who was leading the way, suddenly stopped. His eyes narrowed as he scanned the rocks ahead. "Do you hear that?" he asked, his voice barely above a whisper.

The group fell silent, straining to hear over the roar of the cascades. There it was—a soft, almost imperceptible growl, low and menacing. Before they could react, a shadowy figure leaped from the rocks above, landing with a silent grace and a lethal intent.

The shadow panther was a fearsome sight. Its sleek, black fur seemed to absorb the light, and its eyes glowed with a predatory hunger. It moved with the fluidity of a shadow, blending seamlessly with its surroundings. With a snarl, it lunged at Theo, its claws extended and ready to strike.

Theo managed to block the initial attack with his sword, but the force of the blow knocked him out of balance. He stumbled, and the panther seized the opportunity, its claws raking across his arm. Theo cried out in pain, blood flowing from the deep gashes.

Liam, Ava, and Emma sprang into action. Ava began chanting an incantation, her voice steady despite the fear that gripped her heart. A shimmering barrier formed around Theo, protecting him from the panther's next strike. Emma drew her bow and fired an arrow, aiming for the beast's flank. The arrow struck true, causing the panther to howl in pain and turn its attention toward her.

Liam, armed with his staff, moved to Theo's side, helping him to his feet. "We need to drive it away from here!" he shouted, his eyes never leaving the panther. "Emma, keep it distracted!"

Emma nodded, firing another arrow at the panther. It dodged the shot but hesitated, its eyes flicking between its prey and the source of its pain. Ava continued her chant, the barrier around Theo growing stronger.

Theo, wincing from his injury, tightened his grip on his sword. "I'm not out of this fight yet," he muttered, determination burning in his eyes.

The panther charged at Emma, its movements a blur. She dodged to the side, but the beast was too quick. It swiped at her, its claws grazing her leg and causing her to stumble. Before it could strike again, Theo roared and slashed at its side, his sword cutting through fur and flesh.

The panther turned on Theo, its eyes blazing with fury. Liam stepped forward, his staff glowing with a magical light. He struck the ground, and a wave of energy surged forward, knocking the panther back. It snarled, shaking its head as if trying to clear the daze.

With a combined effort, they pressed on the attack. Emma fired arrow after arrow, her aim deadly accurate despite the pain in her leg. Ava's magic shielded them from the panther's ferocious strikes, and Liam's staff glowed with a protective light, ready to repel any attack.

Theo, bloodied but unbowed, fought with fierce determination. He swung his sword with precision, each strike landing with a force that drove the panther back. Finally, with a coordinated strike from all sides, they managed to wound the beast severely. It let out a final, agonized roar before collapsing onto the rocks, its body going still.

After the Battle

Breathing heavily, the group stood over the fallen panther, their bodies bruised and bloodied but victorious. Liam immediately turned his attention to Theo's wounds, using a healing potion Maeve had given them to staunch the bleeding and promote healing.

"That was close," Theo said, wincing as the potion took effect. "Thanks for having my back."

"Always," Liam replied, his voice filled with relief. "We couldn't do this without each other."

Ava and Emma nodded, their expressions mirroring Liam's sentiment. They had faced many dangers together, but each new challenge only strengthened their bond and their resolve.

After tending to their wounds and catching their breath, they resumed their descent, more cautious now but with a renewed sense of purpose. The jungle seemed to close in all around them, the shadows deeper and the air thicker, but they pressed on, driven by the promise of discovery and the thrill of adventure.

Reaching the Clearing

By the time they reached the bottom of the cascades, the sun was beginning to set, casting a golden glow over the clearing. The ancient stone structures, partially reclaimed by the jungle, stood silent and imposing, their surfaces covered in intricate carvings and creeping vines.

"This is it," Emma said, her voice filled with awe. "The place where the rivers kiss."

Liam consulted the scroll, his eyes scanning the ancient text. "We need to find the next marker," he said. "It should be here, somewhere among these ruins."

They spread out, carefully examining the stone structures and the ground around them. The carvings depicted scenes of the ancient civilizations, their lives, their struggles, and their achievements. It was a glimpse into a world long forgotten, preserved in stone, and waiting to be uncovered.

Ava was the first to find the marker. Hidden among the carvings on a large stone pillar was a symbol identical to the one on the scroll. She called the others over, her excitement palpable.

"This is it," she said, tracing the symbol with her finger. "We're on the right track."

Liam examined the symbol, comparing it to the scroll. "The next piece of the adornment should be here," he said. "We need to find it."

They began to search the area around the pillar, carefully moving aside vines and debris. It was Theo who found the second piece buried under a pile of stones near the base of the pillar. It was another section of the stone adornment, its gold and silver lines glinting in the fading light.

"We did it," Theo said, holding up the piece. "We found the next part."

Emma helps Theo make a necklace with it after they try to match it to the one that Ava holds, but they don't fit yet. With the second piece in hand, they regrouped, their spirits high despite the exhaustion and injuries. They knew their journey was far from over, but each step brought them closer to uncovering the secrets of the ancient civilization and the legendary Sea Train.

As night fell, they set up camp near the cascades, the sounds of the jungle surrounding them. The air was filled with the chorus of nocturnal creatures, and the stars twinkled above, casting a serene glow over the ruins.

Liam, Ava, Emma, and Theo sat around the campfire, the second piece of the adornment lying between them. They compare the symbols of the new stone to the ones in the scroll, and Emma and Ava manage to decipher the next clue. It points to the river basin in the southern-eastern part of the jungle. They knew that more challenges awaited them, but they also knew that together, they could overcome anything.

The adventure continued with new mysteries to solve and new dangers to face. But for now, under the canopy of stars and the watchful eyes of the ancient ruins, they rested, ready to face whatever lay ahead.

Chapter XV:
The Third Leg of The Journey

The Journey Southeast

After resting for several days at the base of the cascades, Liam, Ava, Emma, and Theo felt their strength returning. The jungle had a way of sapping one's energy, but the serene beauty of the cascades and the company of friends had rejuvenated them. With renewed vigor and the second piece of the stone adornment in hand, they prepared to continue their quest.

The symbols on the scroll pointed to a place southeast of their current location, a journey that would take three days through dense jungle terrain. They packed their supplies, checked their weapons, and set off early in the morning, the sunlight filtering through the canopy above.

The jungle seemed both more welcoming and more treacherous than before. The path was uneven, tangled with roots and vines, and the air was thick with humidity. As they moved, the sounds of the jungle accompanied them—the distant calls of birds, the rustle of leaves, and the occasional snap of twigs underfoot.

Liam took the lead, using his knowledge of navigation to keep them on the right path. Ava walked beside him, studying the symbols on the scroll and comparing them to their surroundings. Emma and Theo followed closely, their eyes scanning the jungle for any signs of danger.

Encounter with Man-Eating Plants

On the second day of their journey, the group stumbled upon a section of the jungle that seemed unusually quiet. The usual cacophony of animal sounds was absent, replaced by an eerie silence. The air felt different here, heavier and tinged with a sweet, almost intoxicating scent.

"Stay alert," Emma whispered, her hand resting on the hilt of her sword. "Something's not right."

As they moved cautiously through the area, they began to notice strange, vibrant flowers with petals that shimmered in the dappled sunlight. Their beauty was captivating, but there was something unsettling about them.

Suddenly, one of the flowers moved, its petals unfurling to reveal a gaping maw lined with sharp, thorn-like teeth. Before they could react, vines shot out from the ground, wrapping around Theo's leg and pulling him towards the flower.

"Theo!" Ava screamed, rushing forward with her dagger to cut the vine.

Theo struggled, slashing at the vine with his sword, but more vines began to emerge, wrapping around his arms and legs. Liam and Emma sprang into action, using their weapons to cut through the vines and free their friend.

Ava's incantations provided a magical shield, protecting them from the worst of the vines' attacks. "These plants are carnivorous!" she shouted, her voice filled with urgency. "We need to get out of here!"

The group fought desperately, hacking and slashing at the vines. Theo, finally freed from their grasp, limped away from the flowers, his face pale but determined. "We have to keep moving!" he urged, wincing in pain.

With a combined effort, they managed to cut a path through the jungle, the man-eating plants snapping and thrashing behind them. They didn't stop until they were well clear of the dangerous area, their breaths coming in ragged gasps.

"That was too close," Liam said, his voice shaking. "Is everyone okay?"

"We're fine," Emma replied, though her face was etched with worry. "But we need to be more careful. This jungle is full of surprises."

Ava nodded, her eyes scanning the jungle warily. "Let's keep going. We're getting closer."

Reaching the Destination

By the end of the third day, they reached a large, still body of water surrounded by dense jungle. According to the scroll, their next destination lay on the other side. The water was dark and foreboding, its surface reflecting the dim light of the setting sun.

"We need to cross this," Liam said, looking at the scroll and then at the water. "The next temple is just beyond."

Theo, despite his earlier injury, stepped forward. "I'll go first. We need to find a safe way across."

He waded into the water, moving slowly and cautiously. The others followed, their eyes scanning the surface for any signs of danger. The water was cool, a stark contrast to the humid air, and it rose quickly to their waists.

The Serpent in the Deep

They were halfway across when the water suddenly erupted. A massive serpent, its scales glistening like dark emeralds, burst from the depths. Its eyes were a cold, predatory yellow, and its mouth was filled with rows of razor-sharp teeth.

The beast lunged at Theo, its jaws snapping shut just inches from his face. He threw himself to the side, barely avoiding the attack. The water churned around them, making it difficult to keep their footing.

Liam, Ava, and Emma sprang into action. Ava began chanting an incantation, her voice rising above the chaos, and a shield of shimmering light formed around them, momentarily holding the serpent at bay.

"We need to get to the shore!" Emma shouted, firing arrows at the serpent's eyes. The arrows bounced off its thick scales, but one managed to hit its mark, causing the serpent to hiss in pain and fury.

Theo and Liam moved towards the shore, fighting against the pull of the water. The serpent thrashed, its tail sending waves crashing over them and nearly knocking them off their feet. Ava continued her incantations, maintaining the shield and trying to find a way to weaken the beast.

The serpent lunged again, its jaws snapping shut around the shimmering shield. The force of the attack shattered the shield, sending Ava sprawling into the water. Emma fired another arrow, hitting the serpent's other eye and temporarily blinding it.

Liam reached Ava and helped her to her feet. "We have to distract it," he said, his mind racing. "Emma, keep it busy. Theo and I will try to find its weak spot."

Emma nodded, her focus unwavering despite the chaos. She continued to fire arrows, aiming for the serpent's mouth and eyes. The beast roared, its massive body writhing in pain and anger.

Theo and Liam moved around the serpent, looking for any vulnerable spots. "There!" Theo shouted, pointing to a small gap in the serpent's scales near its head. "That's its weak spot!"

Liam nodded, his mind clear and focused. "We need to hit it together."

As the serpent lunged again, Theo and Liam moved in unison. Theo slashed at the gap with his sword while Liam used a powerful spell to amplify the attack. The combined force of their strikes hit the serpent's weak spot, causing it to convulse violently.

The beast let out a final, ear-piercing roar before collapsing into the water, its body going limp. The water slowly calmed, the serpent's form sinking back into the depths.

The Next Temple

Exhausted and soaked, the group finally made it to the shore. They collapsed on the sandy bank, catching their breath and tending to their injuries.

"That was… intense," Theo said, wincing as he checked the gashes on his leg. "But we did it."

Liam nodded, looking at the scroll. "The next temple should be just ahead."

They gathered their belongings and pressed on, their determination renewed by their victory. As they moved through the dense foliage, the jungle gradually opened up to reveal another ancient temple. This one was larger and more elaborate than the last, its stone walls covered in intricate carvings and adorned with gold and silver accents.

They approached the temple cautiously, their eyes scanning for any signs of danger. The entrance was flanked by statues of ancient warriors, their expressions stern and watchful.

"This is it," Emma said, her voice filled with awe. "The next piece of the adornment must be inside."

Liam, Ava, Theo, and Emma entered the temple, their hearts filled with a mix of excitement and trepidation. The interior was dimly lit, the walls adorned with more carvings depicting the ancient civilization's history and their quest for the Heart of the Ocean.

In the center of the main chamber, on a pedestal, lay the third piece of the stone adornment. It glowed faintly, its gold and silver lines shimmering in the dim light.

"We found it," Ava whispered, her eyes wide with wonder. "The third piece."

Liam carefully picked up the piece, examining it closely. "We're getting closer," he said, his voice steady. "One step at a time."

With the third piece of the adornment in hand, they knew their journey was far from over, but their resolve was stronger than ever. The jungle had tested them, but it had also forged them into a formidable team, ready to face whatever challenges lay ahead.

As they exited the temple, the setting sun casts a warm glow over the ruins. The path ahead was uncertain, but they were ready. Together, they would uncover the secrets of the ancient civilization and the legendary Sea Train, no matter what dangers awaited them.

Chapter XVI:
The Last Stone and The Dungeon Challenge

Liam, Ava, Emma, and Theo made camp at the base of the newly discovered temple. They needed time to rest, recover, and make sense of the third piece of the stone adornment. The jungle, while beautiful, was relentless, and the group had learned the importance of seizing moments of respite when they could.

For two days, they rested in the shadow of the ancient temple, the sounds of the jungle providing a constant backdrop. They took turns keeping watch, wary of any lurking dangers and spent their free time studying the third piece of the adornment and comparing it to the symbols on the scroll.

Liam spread out their findings on a large, flat rock that served as their makeshift table. "We need to figure out where the last piece is," he said, his eyes scanning the intricate lines and symbols.

Ava sat next to him, her fingers tracing the markings. "These symbols here," she said, pointing to a section of the scroll, "they match the ones on this piece. It looks like a map, but it's not complete."

Emma leaned over, her brow furrowed in concentration. "Look at this symbol," she said, pointing to a part of the scroll. "It's repeated here and here, almost like a marker."

Theo, sharpening his sword nearby, glanced over. "What does it say?"

Ava squinted at the ancient script. "It talks about a place east of Mount Eldorian. A dungeon. And a warning about a trial of life or death."

The group exchanged serious looks. They had faced many dangers together, but the mention of a trial of life or death was ominous.

"We have no choice," Liam said, his voice firm. "We need that last piece. If we can get it, we'll be one step closer to finding the Heart of the Ocean and the Sea Train."

They spent the rest of the day preparing for the journey, packing their supplies, and ensuring they were ready for whatever lay ahead. The dense jungle and the unknown trials at Mount Eldorian awaited them.

Journey to Mount Eldorian

The journey to Mount Eldorian took several days. The dense jungle seemed to close in around them, the trees growing taller and the underbrush thicker. The air was humid and heavy, making each step feel like a struggle.

Along the way, they encountered giant spiders, their webs spanning the gaps between trees like silken bridges. The spiders were as large as wolves, their eyes glinting with predatory intent. The group had to move carefully, using fire to drive the spiders away and cutting through the webs with their swords.

One night, as they sat around their campfire, Emma voiced what they were all thinking. "These spiders are getting more aggressive. It's like they know we're here."

Theo nodded, tossing another log onto the fire. "We need to stay sharp. The closer we get to Mount Eldorian, the more dangerous it will become."

Liam and Ava agreed, their minds focused on the trials that awaited them.

The Base of Mount Eldorian

After several days of arduous travel, they reached the eastern base of Mount Eldorian. The mountain loomed above them, its peak shrouded in clouds. The terrain here was rocky and uneven, with jagged cliffs and steep slopes. It was a stark contrast to the lush jungle they had just traversed.

They could see what looked like a rock entrance on the opposite side of their location, partially hidden by the natural formations. Emma took the first steps towards the entrance, her eyes scanning for any signs of danger. She was stopped in her tracks by a familiar hiss.

The Serpent of the Deep, the guardian of the entrance, slithered out from the shadows. Its scales glistened in the dim light, and its eyes glowed with an eerie intelligence. Standing at the entrance of the dungeon, the Serpent of the Deep blocked their path with its massive, coiled body. The group knew that this guardian posed a challenge far greater than any they had faced before.

"Why have you come here, mortals?" the serpent hissed, its voice echoing through the rocky terrain. "What do you seek?"

Emma, her heart pounding in her chest, stepped forward cautiously. "We seek the final piece of the stone adornment," she said, her voice steady despite her fear. "It will lead us to the Heart of the Ocean."

The serpent's eyes narrowed, and it lowered its head to examine them more closely. "Many have sought the Heart of the Ocean," it said, its voice filled with a mix of curiosity and menace. "Few have succeeded. What makes you think you are worthy?"

Liam stepped forward, his eyes meeting the serpent's ones. "We have overcome many challenges to get here," he said. "We are determined to find the Sea Train and uncover the secrets of the ancient civilization."

The serpent regarded them for a moment, its eyes flicking between each member of the group. "Very well," it said finally. "You may attempt the trial. But be warned: it will not be easy. Only the worthy will pass."

"To proceed," the serpent hissed, its voice echoing off the rocky walls, "you must prove your worth through a trial of life or death. Only those who are truly worthy may enter the dungeon and seek the final piece of the stone adornment."

Emma stepped forward, her voice steady despite the fear that gnawed at her insides. "What is this trial? What must we do?"

The serpent regarded them for a moment, its eyes flicking between each member of the group. "The trial is simple yet deadly. Answer my riddle correctly, and you may pass unharmed. Fail, and you will face my wrath, and none shall enter."

Ava, Liam, Theo, and Emma exchanged nervous glances. They had faced countless dangers together, but this was different. The serpent's gaze locked onto them, and it began to recite the riddle:

"I am not alive, but I grow; I don't have lungs, but I need air; I don't have a mouth, and I can drown. What am I?"

The group fell silent, their minds racing to solve the riddle. The weight of the serpent's words pressed upon them, each second feeling like an eternity. Failure meant not just death but the end of their quest.

Theo, wincing from his earlier injury but determined, was the first to speak. "Fire," he said, his voice firm. "The answer is fire."

The serpent's eyes narrowed, and for a moment, the jungle seemed to hold its breath. Then, the serpent uncoiled slightly, allowing a narrow passage to the dungeon entrance. "You have answered correctly," it said, a note of respect in its voice. "You may pass. But remember the trials within are even more perilous. Prove your worth or perish."

The group nodded, the gravity of their situation sinking in. They had passed the first challenge, but the true test awaited them inside the dungeon. As they stepped past the serpent and into the darkness, they knew there was no turning back. They were committed to their quest, no matter the cost.

The serpent watched them disappear into the dungeon, its eyes gleaming with a mixture of respect and curiosity. The trial of life or death had only just begun.

Entering the Dungeon

They entered the dungeon, the air growing cooler and the light dimmer as they descended. The walls were lined with ancient carvings depicting scenes of great battles and powerful magic. The floor was covered in dust, untouched for centuries.

They moved cautiously, their footsteps echoing in the silence. Liam held the torch high, illuminating their path. Ava, Emma, and Theo followed closely, their weapons at the ready.

As they ventured deeper into the dungeon, they encountered various traps and puzzles. Some were mechanical, with gears and levers that needed to be manipulated to open doors or disable traps. Others were magical, requiring Ava's incantations to decipher ancient runes and deactivate enchanted barriers.

At one point, they came across a large chamber filled with statues of ancient warriors. As they stepped into the room, the statues came to life, their stone faces expressionless but their movements swift and deadly.

Theo and Emma took the lead, engaging the statues in combat while Liam and Ava worked to find a way to deactivate them. The battle was fierce, with the statues' stone weapons clashing against their swords and shields. Ava recited an incantation, her voice steady despite the chaos, and the statues slowly began to crumble.

"We're getting closer," Liam said, his eyes scanning the chamber for any clues. "We need to keep moving."

The Guardian's Challenge

Finally, they reached the innermost chamber of the dungeon. In the center of the room, on a raised pedestal, lay the final piece of the stone adornment. But standing between them and the piece was again the Serpent of the Deep.

"You have done well to make it this far," the serpent said, its voice echoing off the stone walls. "But the final trial remains. To claim the piece, you must prove your worth."

The serpent raised its head, its eyes glowing with an intense light. "You must answer this riddle," it said. "Answer correctly, and the piece is yours. Fail, and you will face my wrath."

The group exchanged nervous glances. They had faced many challenges, but a riddle from an ancient guardian was something entirely different.

"Speak the riddle," Liam said, his voice steady.

The serpent's eyes gleamed as it recited the riddle:

"I speak without a mouth and hear without ears. I have no body, but I come alive with the wind. What am I?"

The group fell silent, their minds racing to solve the riddle. Ava was the first to speak. "An echo," she said, her voice confident. "The answer is an echo."

The serpent's eyes narrowed, and for a moment, there was only silence. Then, it lowered its head in a gesture of acknowledgment. "You are correct," it said, but it was not over, as the serpent didn't move out of the way. The serpent coiled itself and transformed into a massive, armored golem with eyes that glowed like molten lava. The guardian's presence was imposing, its stone form radiating an aura of raw power. The air hummed with a palpable energy, and the group knew that this would be their most difficult challenge yet.

Liam, Ava, Emma, and Theo formed a tight circle, their weapons at the ready. The golem's eyes locked onto them, and with a thunderous roar, it charged.

The Battle Begins

Theo met the golem's initial attack head-on, his sword clashing against its stone arm. The force of the impact sent shockwaves through his body, but he held his ground. Emma fired arrows, aiming for the joints in the golem's armor, hoping to find a weak spot. Her arrows struck true, but the golem seemed barely affected.

Liam, wielding his staff, chanted an incantation. A bolt of magical energy shot from the staff, hitting the golem in the chest. The golem staggered but quickly regained its balance, swinging a massive fist towards Liam. Ava stepped in, casting a protective barrier just in time to deflect the blow.

"We need to find its weak spot!" Liam shouted, his eyes darting over the golem's form.

Emma scanned the guardian, noticing a faint glow emanating from the center of its chest. "There!" She pointed. "The core! We need to hit the core!"

A Coordinated Effort

Theo, despite his earlier injury, charged at the golem, distracting it with a flurry of attacks. The golem swung its arms, trying to swat him away, but Theo's agility kept him just out of reach. Emma continued to fire arrows, each one aimed with precision to draw the golem's attention.

Ava and Liam focused their magic, combining their powers to form a single, powerful spell. "On my mark," Liam said, his voice steady despite the chaos. "Now!"

Ava and Liam unleashed a torrent of magical energy aimed directly at the golem's chest. The force of the combined spell hit the core, causing the golem to roar in pain. Its movements became erratic, and cracks began to appear in its stone armor.

Seizing the opportunity, Theo delivered a powerful strike to the golem's leg, causing it to buckle. Emma fired a final arrow, hitting the exposed core. With a deafening roar, the golem collapsed, its body disintegrating into rubble. "We did it," Liam said, his voice filled with relief and pride.

Victory and the Final Stone

The Serpent returned to its original form and said: "You have proven your worth."

With a flick of its tail, the serpent moved aside, allowing them to approach the pedestal.

Panting and exhausted, the group approached the pedestal. The final piece of the stone adornment lay within their grasp. Liam carefully picked it up and examined it closely, a sense of triumph washing over him.

"We did it," Theo said, a smile spreading across his face. "We have all the pieces."

The serpent watched them, its eyes reflecting a mixture of respect and curiosity. "You have done well," it said. "But your journey is far from over. The true test lies ahead."

The group nodded, understanding the gravity of the serpent's words. They had overcome many challenges to reach this point, but the path to the Heart of the Ocean and the Sea Train was still fraught with danger.

Ava, Emma, and Theo gathered around, their faces reflecting a mix of exhaustion and joy. They had faced the guardian and emerged victorious, each of their abilities tested to the limit.

With the final piece in hand, they knew their journey was nearing its climax. The path to the Heart of the Ocean and the legendary Sea Train was now within their reach.

As they left the dungeon, the serpent's parting words echoed in their minds. They had proven their worth, but the true test was yet to come. With the final piece of the stone adornment in hand, they set their sights on the ultimate goal: uncovering the secrets of the ancient civilization and finding the legendary Sea Train.

Their journey had taken them through dense jungles, past dangerous creatures, and into the depths of an ancient dungeon. They had faced trials that tested their strength, intelligence and resolve. But they were ready for whatever lay ahead.

With the final piece of the stone adornment secured, they knew they were one step closer to their goal. The path ahead was uncertain and filled with peril, but their determination was unwavering. Together, they would face whatever challenges awaited them and uncover the secrets of the Heart of the Ocean and the Sea Train.

As they made their way out of the dungeon and back into the light of day, they felt a renewed sense of purpose. The adventure continued, and they were ready for the next chapter of their journey.

Chapter XVII:
Return to Dave's Landing

As Liam, Ava, Emma, and Theo emerged from the dungeon, a breathtaking sunset greeted them at the base of Mount Eldorian. The sky was painted in hues of orange, pink, and gold, casting a serene glow over the rugged landscape. Exhausted but triumphant, they took a moment to savor the view and the sense of accomplishment that came with securing the final piece of the stone adornment.

The group found a suitable spot to set up camp for the night. The air was cool, and the sounds of the jungle were a comforting backdrop as they pitched their tents and built a small fire. Their bodies were weary, but their spirits were high. They had faced numerous challenges and emerged stronger, united by their shared purpose.

Liam spread out one of the maps they had collected during their journey and began tracing a route with his finger. "We need to head east to the land of the giant crabs," he said, his voice thoughtful. "From there, we can find a fishing crew to take us back to Dave's Landing. It'll take us about five days."

Ava, sitting beside him, nodded. "We need to move quickly. The summer months are almost over, and we need to get back to school for our final year."

Emma and Theo joined them, peering over Liam's shoulder at the map. "It'll be an adventure," Emma said with a smile. "I've always wanted to see the giant crabs up close."

Theo grinned, his enthusiasm undimmed despite the day's exertions. "And it'll be a nice change from fighting monsters and navigating ancient traps."

Journey to the East Coast

The next morning, they set off at first light, their packs filled with supplies and their hearts filled with determination. The journey through the jungle was challenging, but the knowledge that they were heading home kept them moving forward. The dense foliage and twisting paths were familiar to them now, each step a testament to their resilience and growing expertise.

As they traveled, they encountered the diverse wildlife of the jungle. Brightly colored birds flitted through the trees, their calls a symphony of the wild. Small animals scurried through the underbrush, and the occasional rustle of leaves hinted at larger creatures watching from a distance.

Arrival at the Coast

After five days of travel, they finally reached the eastern coast. The sight that greeted them was nothing short of magical. The coastline was dotted with sandy beaches and rocky outcrops, the waves gently lapping at the shore. The air was filled with the salty tang of the sea, and the cries of seabirds echoed overhead.

But it was the giant crabs that truly captivated them. These magnificent creatures, each the size of a small car, moved gracefully along the shoreline. Their shells were adorned with patterns of blue and green, reflecting the colors of the ocean. Despite their size, they moved with surprising agility, their pincers snapping at the air with a mixture of curiosity and territoriality.

Ava watched them with wide eyes. "They're beautiful," she whispered, her voice filled with awe.

Emma nodded, equally mesmerized. "And they seem to have their own sense of order. Look how they interact with each other."

Theo, ever the adventurer, couldn't resist moving closer. "Let's get a better look," he said, edging towards a group of crabs. "But carefully. We don't want to provoke them."

The group approached cautiously, observing the crabs from a safe distance. The creatures were indeed territorial, but as long as the group remained respectful of their space, the crabs seemed content to go about their business.

Plans for the Journey Home

As the sun set over the ocean, casting a golden glow over the water, the group made camp on the beach. They sat around a crackling fire, discussing their plans for the journey home.

"We need to find a fishing crew," Liam said, studying the map by the light of the fire. "They'll be able to take us back to Dave's Landing."

Ava nodded. "And once we're back, we can prepare for our final year of school. But we also need to think about what we've discovered. The stone adornment, the Sea Train... there's so much we still need to uncover."

Emma looked thoughtful. "Maybe we can continue our research while we're at school. We can use the library, and there might be scholars who can help us understand more about the ancient civilization."

Theo grinned. "And during breaks, we can plan our next expedition. There's no way we're letting this adventure end here."

The group laughed, the camaraderie that had carried them through so many challenges evident in their shared determination. They had grown closer through their trials, each one bringing their unique strengths to the group and relying on each other to overcome obstacles.

Meeting the Fishing Crew

The next morning, they set out along the coast, keeping an eye out for any signs of fishing crews. It wasn't long before they spotted a small fleet of boats anchored offshore. The fishermen were busy hauling in nets filled with fish and other sea creatures, their voices carrying over the water as they worked.

Liam raised his hand in greeting as they approached. "Hello! We're looking for passage back to Dave's Landing. Can you help us?"

One of the fishermen, a grizzled man with a weather-beaten face, looked up and nodded. "Aye, we can take you. We're heading that way to sell our catch. Hop aboard."

The group climbed into one of the boats, grateful for the opportunity to rest their legs after days of trekking through the jungle. The fishermen were friendly, sharing stories of their adventures at sea and the various creatures they had encountered.

As the boat sailed away from the coast, the group looked back at the land of the giant crabs, its beauty and mystery etched into their memories. The journey had been long and arduous, but it had also been filled with wonder and discovery.

Reflection and Preparation

The voyage back to Dave's Landing took a few hours, the boat cutting smoothly through the waves. The group spent their time reflecting on their journey and planning their next steps. They knew that their adventure was far from over and that the knowledge they had gained would guide them in their future endeavors.

Liam sat with the stone adornment, carefully studying each piece and the symbols inscribed on them. "We still have so much to learn," he said, his voice filled with determination. "But we're on the right path."

Ava nodded, her eyes thoughtful. "And we have each other. Together, we can solve any mystery."

Emma looked out at the horizon, a sense of anticipation in her heart. "Our final year of school will be challenging, but it's also an opportunity. We can use what we've learned to prepare for our next adventure."

Theo grinned, his eyes sparkling with excitement. "And who knows what we'll discover next? The world is full of wonders, and we've only just begun to explore them."

Return to Dave's Landing

When they finally reached Dave's Landing, the bustling port town was a welcome sight. They disembarked from the boat, thanking the fishermen for their help, and made their way through the crowded streets. The familiar sights and sounds of the town filled them with a sense of homecoming.

As they walked towards their home (the Sailor's Rest), the weight of their journey settled over them. They had faced countless challenges, discovered ancient secrets, and forged unbreakable bonds. Their adventure had changed them, each one emerging stronger and more determined.

As they prepared to start their final year of school, they knew that their journey was far from over. The mysteries of the Sea Train and the Heart of the Ocean awaited them, and they were ready to face whatever challenges lay ahead.

Together, they would uncover the secrets of the past and pave the way for a future filled with adventure and discovery. The world was vast and full of wonders, and Liam, Ava, Emma, and Theo were ready to explore every corner of it.

The Final Part:

The last challenges, the fish people, the sea serpent, and the Sea Train

Chapter XVIII
The Harvest Festival

Several months had passed since Liam, Ava, Emma, and Theo had returned to Dave's Landing. The small coastal city was now alive with preparations for the Harvest Festival, a grand celebration that marked the end of the harvest season and the last days of autumn. The streets were adorned with colorful banners, stalls were set up with local produce and crafts, and the air was filled with the smell of roasted chestnuts and spiced cider.

Amidst the festive atmosphere, Liam and his friends remained focused on their quest. They had spent countless hours poring over the pieces of the stone adornment, deciphering the symbols, and trying to piece together the puzzle. Despite their progress, it seemed that a crucial center piece was still missing.

Liam spread the stones out on a table in the library, his brow furrowed in concentration. "We're so close," he said, frustration evident in his voice. "But it feels like we're missing something vital."

Ava, seated next to him with a notebook filled with translations and notes, nodded in agreement. "It's like there's a gap in the center, something that ties all these pieces together."

Emma looked thoughtful. "Maybe Maeve can help. She's the one who got us started on this path. She might know something we don't."

Theo grinned, his eyes lighting up with excitement. "And the festival is the perfect time to visit her shop. Let's go see her."

Visiting Maeve During the Festival

The streets of Dave's Landing were bustling with people enjoying the Harvest Festival. Musicians played lively tunes, children ran about with colorful ribbons, and vendors shouted out their wares. The group made their way through the crowd, their destination clear in their minds.

Maeve's shop, "Maeve's Curiosities," was tucked away in a quiet corner at the back of the market. The familiar bell chimed as they entered, and the scent of incense and herbs filled the air. Maeve looked up from a book she was reading behind the counter and smiled warmly.

"Welcome, my friends," she greeted them. "I had a feeling you'd be back."

Liam stepped forward, the stones in his hands. "Maeve, we've made progress, but we're missing something. We need your help to complete the puzzle."

Maeve's eyes twinkled with curiosity as she examined the stones. "Let's see what you've discovered."

The Missing Piece

Maeve spread the stones out on the counter and carefully studied the symbols. Her fingers traced the intricate lines, and she murmured softly to herself. After a few moments, she looked up at the group, a thoughtful expression on her face.

"You've done well," she said, "but you're right. There's a piece missing—a small center piece that connects all the others."

Liam nodded eagerly. "Do you know what it is or where we can find it?"

Maeve smiled enigmatically. "I believe I do. The missing piece is a key, literally and figuratively. It's said to be located in the heart of the land of the giant crabs, where the ancient civilization hid it to protect their secrets."

Emma's eyes widened. "We were just there! How did we miss it?"

"The land of the giant crabs is vast," Maeve explained. "The key is hidden in a sacred grove known only to a few. The crabs are guardians of the grove, and only those who show respect and understanding can access it."

Theo's excitement was palpable. "So, we need to go back and find this grove. Any advice on how to approach the crabs?"

Maeve nodded. "The giant crabs are territorial but not unkind. Approach them with offerings from the sea—shellfish and kelp. Show them you mean no harm, and they will guide you to the grove."

Ava looked determined. "We need to prepare. This is our chance to complete the puzzle and unlock the secrets of the Sea Train."

Maeve placed a reassuring hand on Ava's shoulder. "You've come a long way, and I have faith in you. Remember, the journey is as important as the destination. Trust in each other and in what you've learned."

Preparing for the Journey

The group spent the rest of the festival gathering supplies and making preparations for their return to the land of the giant crabs. They plan on going to the area after their fall finals and use grandpa's boat to get there. They visited the market stalls, trading for fresh shellfish and bundles of kelp, knowing that these offerings would be crucial for gaining the crabs' trust.

As night fell and the festival lights illuminated the town, they gathered in the library one last time to review their plan. Liam spread out the map, pointing to their route.

"We'll take the path through the coast, as it would be faster than going again through the jungle," he said, "but this time, we'll be looking for signs of the sacred grove. Keep an eye out for any unusual markings or paths."

Emma nodded. "And we need to be respectful and careful around the crabs. They're the key to finding the grove."

Theo grinned, his confidence evident. "We've faced tougher challenges. We can do this."

Ava looked around at her friends, a sense of pride and determination filling her. "Let's get some rest. We have a long journey ahead."

The Return to the Land of the Giant Crabs

Several days later, at dawn, they set out once more, their packs filled with supplies and their hearts filled with determination. The ocean seemed almost welcoming at this time, the familiar sounds and sights providing a sense of déjà vu. The journey was challenging, but they moved with purpose, driven by the knowledge that they were close to uncovering the final piece of the puzzle.

After several hours of travel, they reached the eastern coast once again. The sight of the giant crabs moving gracefully along the shoreline brought a sense of excitement and anticipation. They approached the crabs cautiously, their offerings held out in front of them.

The crabs paused in their movements, their eyes locking onto the group. Slowly, they moved forward, their pincers gently accepting the offerings. The crabs' demeanor changed. Their movements became less aggressive and more inquisitive.

Liam stepped forward, speaking softly. "We seek the sacred grove, the heart of your land. Can you guide us?"

One of the largest crabs, its shell adorned with intricate patterns, seemed to understand. It clicked its pincers and began to move, leading the group along the shoreline. The other crabs followed, creating a protective circle around them.

Discovering the Sacred Grove

The journey through the land of the giant crabs was awe-inspiring. The crabs moved with a grace and intelligence that spoke of their ancient guardianship. The group followed their guide through rocky outcrops and hidden pathways until they reached a secluded grove, its entrance marked by a natural archway of coral and seaweed.

The grove was a place of serene beauty, with crystal-clear pools and lush vegetation. At the center of the grove, on a raised platform of stone and coral, lay the missing piece of the stone adornment. It glowed with a soft, ethereal light as if waiting for their arrival.

Ava stepped forward, her heart pounding with excitement. She carefully picked up the piece, feeling a sense of completion and triumph. "We did it," she whispered, her eyes shining.

Liam, Emma, and Theo gathered around, their expressions filled with awe and pride. They had faced countless challenges, but their determination and unity had brought them to this moment.

The Puzzle Completed

Back at the boat, they assembled the pieces of the stone adornment, the final piece fitting perfectly into place. The symbols glowed brightly; their meaning was now clear. The adornment was a key, a map, and a guide to the Heart of the Ocean and the Sea Train.

"We need to decipher the final instructions," Liam said, his voice filled with anticipation. "This will lead us to the Sea Train."

Maeve's words echoed in their minds: Trust in each other and in what you've learned. They knew that their journey was far from over, but they were ready to face whatever challenges lay ahead.

As the sun set over the land of the giant crabs, casting a golden glow over the ocean, the group felt a renewed sense of purpose. They had completed the puzzle, but the adventure continued. Together, they would unlock the secrets of the ancient civilization and uncover the mysteries of the Sea Train.

With the final piece of the stone adornment in hand and the path ahead illuminated, Liam, Ava, Emma, and Theo prepared for the next chapter of their journey. The world was vast and full of wonders, and they were ready to explore every corner of it, united by their quest and the bonds of friendship that had grown stronger with each step of their adventure.

Chapter XIX:
The Search for the Sea Train

With school finally behind them, Liam, Ava, Emma, and Theo felt a mix of relief and anticipation. They had all graduated with high marks, and in the case of Ava and Theo ahead of time, their academic achievements were underscored by the incredible adventures they had shared. But now, the real journey awaited them. With all the pieces of the stone puzzle in hand and the blessings of their parents, they knew it was time to return to Maeve for the final translation and to uncover the location of the Sea Train.

Maeve welcomed them warmly into her shop, her eyes twinkling with the same curiosity and wisdom they had come to respect. The stone adornment pieces were spread out on her counter, glowing faintly with an ancient light. She examined them closely, her fingers tracing the symbols with practiced ease.

"This is a remarkable achievement," Maeve said, her voice filled with genuine admiration. "You've managed to find and assemble all the pieces. Now, let's see what secrets they hold."

The Translation

Maeve began to chant softly, an ancient incantation that filled the room with a sense of timelessness. The symbols on the stone pieces started to glow brighter, the light weaving together to form a coherent pattern. As the light settled, the message became clear, and Maeve translated it aloud.

"The stones speak of a hidden door north of Aeloria's coast, by the northern cliffs," she said, her eyes focused and intense. "It's a place known only to a few, guarded by natural and magical defenses. The Sea Train lies beyond that door, in a sanctuary created by the ancient civilization."

Liam, Ava, Emma, and Theo listened intently, their hearts pounding with excitement. The mention of the northern cliffs brought to mind a rugged and isolated part of the coastline, a place shrouded in mystery and often spoken of in local legends.

"This is it," Liam said, his voice filled with awe. "We're so close."

Maeve nodded. "But be warned, the journey to the northern cliffs is fraught with danger. The hidden door is well protected, and only those who prove their worth can gain access."

Preparation for the Journey

Determined to face whatever challenges lay ahead, the group began their preparations. They gathered supplies, checked their weapons, and studied maps of Aeloria's northern coast. The journey would be long (several days through rough waters) and treacherous, but their resolve was unwavering.

Emma, ever the strategist, plotted their route. "We'll need to travel by sea to reach the northern cliffs. The terrain is too rough for overland travel, and the waters can be unpredictable."

Theo grinned, his adventurous spirit undimmed. "Sounds perfect. Let's find a boat and set sail."

Setting Sail

The group secured passage on a sturdy vessel captained by a seasoned sailor named Captain AJ Harwin. The captain was a grizzled old man with a wealth of knowledge about the northern waters and the dangers they presented.

"You're a brave lot, heading to the northern cliffs," Captain Harwin said as they set sail. "Those waters are treacherous, and the cliffs themselves are known for their deadly beauty. But if anyone can make it, it's you four."

The journey by sea was both exhilarating and challenging. The waves crashed against the hull of the ship, and the wind whipped through their hair. The vast expanse of the ocean stretched out before them, a reminder of the adventure that awaited.

The Northern Cliffs

After several days at sea, the northern cliffs came into view. They rose majestically from the water, their rugged edges and towering heights casting long shadows in the early morning light. The cliffs were as beautiful as they were intimidating, with waves crashing against their base and seabirds circling above.

Captain Harwin guided the ship to a small cove, where the group disembarked. "This is as far as I can take you," he said. "The rest is up to you. Good luck, and may the winds be in your favor."

Liam, Ava, Emma, and Theo thanked the captain and began their ascent. The path up the cliffs was steep and narrow, requiring every bit of their strength and agility. The air grew cooler as they climbed, the sound of the crashing waves growing fainter.

The Hidden Door

At the top of the cliffs, they found themselves in a windswept landscape of jagged rocks and sparse vegetation. The view was breathtaking, with the ocean stretching out to the horizon. But their focus was on finding the hidden door, the key to the Sea Train.

Using the stone adornment as a guide, they searched for any signs of the door. The symbols on the stones glowed faintly, leading them to a secluded spot where the cliff face appeared unremarkable. Liam ran his fingers over the rock, feeling for any hidden mechanisms.

"Here," he said, his voice filled with excitement. "There's something here."

Ava stepped forward, reciting an incantation she had learned from Maeve. The rock face shimmered, revealing an ornate door covered in ancient symbols. The door was made of a material that seemed to pulse with energy, a testament to the advanced knowledge of the ancient civilization.

The Guardian's Test

As they approached the door, a figure emerged from the shadows. It was an ethereal being, its form shifting and shimmering like mist. The guardian of the door regarded them with eyes that glowed with an otherworldly light.

"To pass through this door," the guardian said, its voice resonating with power, "you must prove your worth. Answer my riddle, and you may proceed. Fail, and you will be turned away."

The group exchanged nervous glances, their minds racing. They had faced riddles and tests before, but this felt different— more significant.

The Guardian spoke the riddle:

"I am the beginning of eternity, the end of time and space, the beginning of every end, and the end of every place. What am I?"

They fell silent, their thoughts whirling. The riddle was cryptic, its meaning elusive. Ava, her mind sharp and analytical, considered the words carefully. Suddenly, her eyes lit up with understanding.

"The letter 'E,'" she said confidently. "The answer is the letter 'E'."

The guardian's eyes glowed brighter for a moment, then it nodded. "You have answered correctly. You may pass."

Entering the Sanctuary

The door opened with a soft, resonant hum, revealing a passageway that led deep into the cliffs. The air inside was cool and filled with the scent of ancient stone and hidden secrets. The group stepped through the doorway, their hearts pounding with anticipation.

The passageway led them to a vast underground chamber illuminated by a soft, otherworldly light. The walls were covered in intricate carvings and glowing symbols depicting the history and achievements of the ancient civilization. At the center of the chamber, a raised platform lay, but there was no sign of the Sea Train. Instead, they found an intricate door with cryptic engravings, ancient symbols, and a riddle inscribed on its surface:

"To pass this door and claim the prize, Answer the questions where wisdom lies. Seek the one who guards the deep. In her riddles, the key does sleep."

{The inscription hinted at the Sea Serpent, a legendary creature of Aeloria. The fourth stood puzzled, the sea breeze rustling through the ceiling above them.}

"Who or what is this guardian?" Emma asked, her brow furrowed.

"And where can we find it...or him/her?" Theo added, glancing around as if expecting the creature to appear.

Liam rubbed his chin thoughtfully. "Maeve might know. She seems to have answers for everything. Let's head back to Dave's Landing and ask her."

Back in Dave's Landing, the market bustled with its usual energy. The aroma of freshly baked goods from Liam's mother's kitchen filled the air, mingling with the salty sea breeze. Liam, Emma, Ava, and Theo hurried to Maeve's stall, their minds abuzz with questions.

Maeve looked up from her assortment of mystical trinkets and potions as they approached. "Back so soon, young adventurers?" she asked, her eyes twinkling with knowing.

Liam presented the riddle. "We need to find the guardian of the deep Sea to answer these questions. Do you know where we can find him or her?"

Maeve's expression grew serious. "The one you speak of is the Sea Serpent. The Sea Serpent is not just any creature, Liam. She is the guardian of the island's secrets, a being of great wisdom and power. She resides in the Heart of the Sea, a hidden grotto beneath the waves, accessible only to those who are worthy."

Ava, Emma, and Theo exchanged glances, all apprehensive and excited said in unison, "How do we prove ourselves worthy?" "Have we not shown that already?".

Maeve gestured to a small, intricately carved box on her table. "Take this. It's an ancient relic passed down through generations.

It will guide you to the Heart of the Sea. Remember, the Serpent tests not just your knowledge but your character. Be honest, be brave, and most importantly, be true to yourselves."

Armed with the relic, they set off once more, this time to the shores where the jungle met the ocean by the southeastern shore of the island. The relic, a beautifully carved conch shell, began to glow faintly as they approached those waters. Following its light, they waded into the sea, feeling the cool water rise around them.

To their astonishment, the water parted, revealing a hidden path beneath the waves. They followed the path, descending deeper into the ocean until they reached a hidden grotto illuminated by bioluminescent plants and glowing corals. Liam tells everyone to drink Maeve's potion as a precaution since they are going to descend into the mysterious underwater grotto. It is here (after they drink the position) that they meet the first fish people.

Chapter XX:
The Fish People and their Underwater City.

As they descended into the grotto, the dim light from above gave way to a mesmerizing display of bioluminescent plants and corals. The walls of the grotto were alive with a soft, glowing blue and green light, casting an ethereal glow over everything. It was a stunning and otherworldly sight as if they had entered a hidden paradise.

The water around them was crystal clear, and schools of vibrant fish darted about, their scales shimmering in the bioluminescent light. It was then that they noticed they were not alone. A group of fish people, their bodies sleek and shimmering, emerged from the depths. They had an otherworldly beauty, with skin that glowed faintly and scales that reflected the colors of the coral. Their eyes were large and luminous, giving them an eerie yet captivating appearance. They moved gracefully through the water, their movements synchronized and fluid.

One of the fish people, who seemed to be the leader, swam forward and gestured for the group to follow. Despite their initial surprise, Liam, Ava, Emma, and Theo felt a sense of calm and trust emanating from the fish people. They decided to follow, curious to learn more about these mysterious beings.

The Underwater City

The fish people led them deeper into the grotto, and soon, the underwater city came into view. It was a breathtaking sight, with buildings made of coral and stone glowing softly in the bioluminescent light. The architecture was intricate and elegant, with arches and spires that seemed to blend seamlessly with the natural surroundings.

As they entered the city, they were greeted by more fish people, all of whom seemed to be expecting them. The city was bustling with activity, with fish people going about their daily lives, tending to gardens of underwater plants, and crafting beautiful items from shells and coral.

The leader of the fish people led them to a grand palace at the center of the city. The palace was a magnificent structure, its walls adorned with intricate carvings and glowing coral. They were guided through a series of grand hallways until they reached the throne room.

Meeting the Ruler

The throne room was a vast, open space with high ceilings and walls covered in bioluminescent plants. At the far end of the room sat the ruler of the fish people on a throne made of coral and shells. The ruler was a regal figure with an aura of wisdom and authority. Their scales glowed with a soft, golden light, and their eyes were a deep ocean blue.

The leader of the fish people introduced the group to the ruler. "These are the travelers from the surface, those who seek the secrets of the ancient civilization and the Sea Train."

The ruler regarded them with a thoughtful expression, their eyes studying each member of the group. "Welcome to our city," the ruler said, their voice resonating with a gentle power. "We have been expecting you."

Liam stepped forward, his voice respectful but filled with curiosity. "We are honored to be here. We seek the secrets of the

Sea Train and the ancient civilization that once thrived on this island."

The ruler nodded. "You have come far and faced many challenges. The Sea Train is a sacred relic, and its secrets are closely guarded. But you have proven your worth by reaching our city."

Ava spoke up, her voice filled with determination. "We are committed to uncovering the truth and understanding the legacy of the ancient civilization. We seek your guidance."

The Princess's Commitment

The ruler smiled with a warm and welcoming expression. "You will find what you seek, but first, there is someone I would like you to meet."

At that moment, a young fish woman entered the throne room. She was beautiful, with scales that shimmered like silver and eyes that glowed with a vibrant green light. She moved with grace and confidence, her presence commanding attention.

"This is my daughter, Princess Vivi," the ruler said. "She has been preparing for this moment, and she will guide you to the sacred caves where the final secrets of the Sea Train are kept."

Princess Vivi stepped forward and bowed slightly. "It is an honor to meet you," she said, her voice clear and melodic. (Princess Vivi was close in age to Emma and Liam, roughly 19 or 20 years old.) "I have studied the ancient texts and know the path to the sacred caves. I will guide you and ensure you find what you seek."

Emma looked at the princess with admiration. "We are grateful for your help, Princess Vivi. This means a lot to us."

Theo grinned. "With your guidance, we're sure to uncover the secrets of the Sea Train."

The Journey to the Sacred Caves

Princess Vivi led the group out of the palace and through the city, explaining the history and culture of her people as they went. "Our ancestors were part of the ancient civilization that once thrived on the island," she said. "When the great cataclysm came, they adapted to life underwater, preserving their knowledge and traditions."

As they reached the edge of the city, they entered a series of tunnels that led deeper into the underwater landscape. The tunnels were illuminated by bioluminescent plants, casting a soft, otherworldly glow that guided their way.

"The sacred caves are hidden deep within these tunnels," Princess Vivi explained. "They are protected by powerful magic, and only those who are worthy can enter."

The journey through the tunnels was both beautiful and eerie. The walls were covered in glowing plants and intricate carvings that told the story of the ancient civilization. The air was filled with the gentle sound of water and the occasional distant echo.

As they ventured deeper, they encountered various challenges that tested their abilities. At one point, they had to solve a complex puzzle involving ancient symbols and mechanisms. Liam and Ava worked together, using their knowledge of the ancient language to decipher the clues and unlock the passage.

Further along, they faced a trial of combat, where they had to defend themselves against guardian creatures that emerged from the shadows. Theo and Emma fought bravely, their skills honed by their previous adventures, and managed to overcome the guardians with the help of Princess Vivi's guidance.

The Sacred Caves

Finally, they reached the entrance to the sacred caves. The entrance was marked by a grand archway made of glowing coral, and the air was thick with a sense of ancient power. Princess Vivi stepped forward and recited an incantation, causing the archway to shimmer and open, revealing the path to the inner sanctum.

The sacred caves were a sight to behold. The walls were lined with glowing crystals and intricate carvings that depicted the history and achievements of the ancient civilization. Suddenly, the environment at the inner sanctum changed, and the Sea Serpent appeared. Her eyes opened, revealing depths of ancient wisdom. She rose, her scales shimmering in the underwater light. "Why have you come, young ones?" her voice echoed through the water, both gentle and powerful.

Liam stepped forward, heart pounding. "We seek the key to unlock the door that leads to the Sea Train. We are here to answer your riddles."

The Sea Serpent regarded them with a long, thoughtful gaze. "Very well. Answer these riddles, and you shall have what you seek."

Her voice resonated through the sanctum as she began:

"The more you take, the more you leave behind. What am I?"

Emma, ever quick with words, whispered, "Footsteps." The Sea Serpent nodded approvingly.

"I have cities but no houses. I have mountains but no trees. I have water but no fish. What am I?"

Theo, the strategist, thought for a moment before replying, "A map." The Serpent's eyes glowed brighter.

"I am easy to lift but hard to throw. What am I?"

Liam pondered, recalling the times he spent tending to his shores at home. "A feather," he answered confidently.

The Sea Serpent let out a melodious laugh. "You have answered well. But there is one final question, the most important of all: What is the true treasure you seek?"

Liam, Emma, Ava, and Theo looked at each other. Finally, Liam spoke, "It's not just the Sea Train or the adventures. It's the bonds we share, the courage we find within ourselves, and the wisdom we gain along the way."

The Sea Serpent nodded, her eyes full of approval. "You have proven yourselves worthy. The key is not just a thing (key) but also the realization of your own strengths and the power of your friendship. Go, and you shall find the way." The serpent disappeared after that.

At the center of the main chamber stood a pedestal, upon which lay a crystal key pulsating with a soft, blue light.

"This is the key to the Sea Train," Princess Vivi said, her voice filled with reverence. "It will unlock the final secrets and allow you to access its full potential."

Liam carefully picked up the crystal key, feeling its power resonate through him. "We've come so far," he said, his voice filled with awe. "This key will unlock the knowledge we've been seeking."

The Exchange with the Ruler

With the crystal key in hand and the serpent's blessing, the group returned to the city and the throne room. The ruler greeted them with a proud smile. "You have proven your worth and earned the right to unlock the secrets of the Sea Train," they said. "But remember, with great knowledge comes great responsibility. Use it wisely."

Liam nodded. "We understand. We will honor the legacy of the ancient civilization and use this knowledge to help others."

Ava stepped forward. "We are grateful for your guidance and for allowing us to uncover these secrets. We will not take this responsibility lightly."

Emma looked at Princess Vivi. "Thank you for your help. We couldn't have done this without you."

Theo grinned. "This is just the beginning. With the Sea Train, we can explore so much more and uncover even greater mysteries."

Princess Vivi smiled. "It has been an honor to help you. I have faith that you will use this knowledge for good."

As they prepared to leave the underwater city, the group felt a deep sense of accomplishment and anticipation. They had unlocked the final secrets of the Sea Train and gained the crystal key that would allow them to access it. With the crystal key in hand, they boarded a vessel that was provided to them by the ruler. As the vessel hummed to life, they felt a sense of exhilaration and readiness for the journey ahead. The vessel began to move, gliding smoothly along its tracks and heading towards the surface. The underwater city grew smaller in the distance, a hidden paradise that had revealed its secrets to those who were worthy and now to them.

As they emerged from the grotto and into the sunlight, the group looked out at the horizon, their hearts filled with the thrill of discovery and the promise of new adventures. The Sea Train was not just a relic of the past; it was a gateway to the future, a means to explore the world and uncover its hidden wonders.

Liam, Ava, Emma, and Theo stood together, united by their shared quest and the bonds of friendship that had grown stronger with each challenge they faced. They knew that the journey ahead would be filled with both dangers and wonders, but they were ready to face whatever lay ahead.

With the crystal key and the knowledge they had gained, they set their sights on the next chapter of their adventure. The world was vast and full of mysteries, and they were determined to explore every corner of it. Liam, Ava, Emma, and Theo were ready to embrace it with open hearts and minds, and together, they would uncover the secrets of the past and pave the way for a future filled with discovery and wonder.

Chapter XXI:
Unlocking The Door

After a few days resting at home, they returned to the stone door. As they approached, the symbols on the map and the engravings on the door began to glow, resonating with newfound energy (the stone, the key, and their inner realization of their own strengths and the power of friendships). Liam stepped forward and placed his hand on the door.

"I am Liam," he said, "and we seek the Sea Train not for glory but for the adventure and the bonds we share."

The door rumbled the ancient mechanisms within coming to life. Slowly, it swung open, revealing a hidden cavern where the legendary Sea Train rested, shimmering with an ethereal glow. The Sea Train was a marvel of engineering and beauty. Its sleek, streamlined form was made of materials that seemed to shimmer with an inner light, and it was as big as a galleon or even bigger. It was a vessel that could go on water and air. It rested on tracks that disappeared into a tunnel that led to the ocean, but it also seemed that it connected with the air, hinting at the vast networks it connected, and it could travel.

Liam, Ava, Emma, and Theo approached the Sea Train with a mix of awe and reverence.

They stepped inside, their hearts filled with awe and excitement. The journey had tested their bravery, their friendship, and their wisdom, but they had emerged stronger and closer than ever before. They had journeyed far and faced countless challenges to reach this point. The Sea Train represented the culmination of their quest and the key to unlocking the secrets of the ancient civilization.

And so, Liam, Emma, Ava, and Theo embarked on the adventure of a lifetime and boarded the mystical Sea Train, ready to explore its wonders and the mysteries beyond their island home of Aeloria.

The Journey Ahead

As they examined the Sea Train, they found a control panel with symbols that matched those on the stone adornments and even a place for the crystal key. Liam carefully placed the completed adornment and the key into the slots on the panel. The symbols lit up, and the Sea Train hummed to life, its engines purring softly.

"This is incredible," Emma said, her eyes wide with wonder. "We've actually found it."

Theo grinned, his excitement palpable. "And now we can explore the ancient civilization's network. Who knows what other secrets and treasures are out there?"

Ava looked thoughtful. "We've come so far, but this is just the beginning. The Sea Train can take us to places we've only dreamed of, places filled with knowledge and history."

Liam nodded, his eyes reflecting the determination that had carried them through their journey. "We need to continue our quest. The Sea Train is a key to understanding the past and shaping the future. Let's see where it takes us." After saying those words, the crew that commanded the Sea Train showed up from below. It was a mixture of different races, all proven loyal, knowledgeable, and strong. The fourth of them stood quietly and surprised, their expressions presenting a notion that asked the question: "What now?"

Chapter XXII:
The Crew That Commanded and Care for The Sea Train

Liam, Ava, Emma, and Theo stood speechless as the Sea Train glided smoothly through the water, and a group of men emerged from the cabins below. The men were a diverse collection of species, each with human characteristics but also distinct marine-like features. Despite their unusual appearances, they all seemed friendly and welcoming.

Leading the group was their captain, David, a fishman from Atlantis. David was an impressive figure, tall and strong, with scales that shined like gold flakes when the light reflected on them. His hair took on the colors of the setting sun, a brilliant blend of oranges, pinks, and purples that shimmered as he moved. His eyes were a deep ocean blue, filled with wisdom and warmth.

David's voice was as deep and resonant as the ocean depths, a testament to his origin. "Greetings, champions," he said with a bow, his golden scales glinting in the sunlight. "I am Captain David of the Sea Train, and these are my companions. We are honored to have you join us." He gestured towards the crew standing behind him.

Liam, Ava, Emma, and Theo took a moment to absorb the sight before them. The crew was an eclectic mix of beings, each with unique characteristics that hinted at their marine heritage. There was a tall, lithe woman with hair like seaweed, eyes that shimmered like pearls, and webbed fingers; a burly man with skin that resembled shark hide, a perpetually stern expression, and teeth that gleamed sharply whenever he spoke; and a smaller, more agile individual with octopus-like tentacles for arms, who moved with a grace that belied their unusual appendages.

Liam, finding his voice, stepped forward. "Thank you, Captain David. We are Liam, Ava, Emma, and Theo. We've come a long way to uncover the secrets of the Sea Train and the ancient civilization."

David smiled a friendly and reassuring expression. "We know of your journey. The Sea Train has been waiting for those worthy of its secrets. Allow me to introduce you to the crew," David continued. "This is Marina," he said, pointing to the woman with seaweed hair. "She is our navigator and possesses an unparalleled sense of direction. Next to her is Balthazar, our enforcer. His strength is unmatched, and he ensures the safety of our vessel. And finally, this is Zephyr," he indicated to the tentacled crew member. "Zephyr is our engineer, a master of mechanics and technology."

Marina stepped forward first, her movements fluid and graceful. "Welcome aboard," she said, her voice soft but carrying the weight of the ocean's wisdom. "It's an honor to serve alongside the new champions of the Sea Train."

Balthazar grunted in agreement, his expression softening slightly. "We'll keep this ship running smoothly and protect it with our lives," he said, his voice rough but sincere.

Zephyr waved a tentacle in greeting, a broad smile on their face. "I've been looking forward to meeting you all! There's so much we can achieve together," they said enthusiastically.

Liam, Ava, Emma, and Theo exchanged glances, their initial shock slowly giving way to excitement. They had been chosen as the new champions and captains of the Sea Train. This responsibility was both daunting and exhilarating.

"Thank you for your warm welcome," Ava said, stepping forward. "We're eager to learn more about the Sea Train and how we can help. What exactly does being a champion entail?"

David smiled, his golden scales catching the light once more. "As champions, you will lead us on our journeys, make critical decisions, and ensure that the Sea Train fulfills its mission. We travel the seas, connecting distant lands, aiding those in need, and protecting the oceans from threats. It's a noble cause, but it requires courage, wisdom, and teamwork."

Emma nodded thoughtfully. "It sounds like a great adventure. We're ready to take on this challenge."

Theo, who had been quiet until now, spoke up. "What kind of threats do we face? And how do we prepare for them?"

Balthazar crossed his arms over his chest, his expression serious. "The seas are filled with dangers—pirates, sea monsters, and even dark sorcery. We train constantly to stay sharp and ready for anything. You'll need to do the same."

Zephyr added, "And don't forget about the mechanical side of things. The Sea Train is a marvel of technology, but it needs constant maintenance and upgrades. I'll teach you everything you need to know."

David placed a reassuring hand on Theo's shoulder. "You'll have the full support of the crew. Together, we'll face any challenge that comes our way."

The rest of the Crew

David gestured to the rest of the men around him, who stepped forward one by one to introduce themselves. Each again had unique features that reflected their marine heritage.

First was Rylan, a burly man with the powerful build of a deep-sea diver. His skin had a slight blue tint, and gill-like slits on his neck hinted at his ability to breathe underwater. His eyes were a striking silver, and he radiated strength and reliability.

Next was Nereus, a slender, graceful figure with webbed fingers and toes. His skin was smooth and iridescent, with a faint luminescence that made him appear ethereal. Nereus had an air of calm and wisdom, and his movements were fluid and precise.

Following Nereus was Talia, a woman with the sharp features and agile build of a predator of the deep. Her eyes were a piercing green, and her dark hair flowed like seaweed. She had faint stripes on her skin, reminiscent of a tiger shark, and an air of fierce determination.

Then came Kai, a young man with a playful grin and the quick, darting movements of a fish. His skin had a mottled pattern of blue and green, and his hair was a tousled mess that looked like it was always wet. Kai exuded energy and enthusiasm, a stark contrast to the serene Nereus.

Finally, there was Lyra, a woman with a regal bearing and an aura of mystery. Her scales were a deep, iridescent purple, and her eyes were a striking amber. She wore intricate jewelry made from seashells and coral, and she had an air of authority that commanded respect. Lyra was also the cook of the sea train, and her cooking was always praised by the rest of them.

Offering Their Services

Captain David turned to the group. "We are at your service. The Sea Train is a marvel of ancient technology, and we are its guardians. We will help you uncover its secrets and guide you on your journey."

Theo's eyes sparkled with excitement. "This is incredible! I appreciate your help. We've been through so much to get here, and we can't wait to see what the Sea Train can do."

Ava nodded in agreement. "We appreciate your offer. There's so much we want to learn, and having your guidance will make a huge difference."

David smiled. "Come, let me show you around the Sea Train and introduce you to its wonders."

The Wonders of the Sea Train

David led them through the corridors of the Sea Train, pointing out various features and explaining their functions. The walls were adorned with glowing symbols and intricate carvings that depicted the history and achievements of the ancient civilization.

"The Sea Train is powered by a rare crystal known as the Heart of the Ocean," David explained, gesturing to a glowing crystal embedded in the control panel. "It provides endless energy and allows the train to travel vast distances underwater, in the air, or on land (if needed)."

As they moved deeper into the train, they reached the observation deck, a large chamber with transparent walls that provided a breathtaking view of the underwater world. Schools of colorful fish swam by, and the light filtered through the water, creating a mesmerizing dance of shadows and colors.

"This is beautiful," Emma said, her voice filled with awe. "I've never seen anything like it."

David nodded. "The observation deck is one of the many wonders of the Sea Train. It was designed to showcase the beauty of the ocean and remind us of the importance of preserving it."

Next, they visited the engine room, where Zephyr (helped by Rylan and Talia) explained the intricate workings of the train's propulsion system. "The Sea Train uses a combination of advanced technology and magic to navigate the ocean depths," Zephyr said. "It's a delicate balance, but it allows us to travel quickly and efficiently."

Talia added, "We also have a sophisticated navigation system that helps us avoid hazards and find the safest routes."

The Library and Archives

David then led them to the library and archives, a vast room filled with ancient scrolls, books, and artifacts. Lyra and Nereus were the custodians of this knowledge, and they eagerly shared their expertise.

"This library contains the accumulated wisdom of our ancestors," Lyra said, her voice reverent. "It's a treasure trove of knowledge about the ancient civilization, their technology, and their culture."

Nereus nodded. "We've been preserving and studying these texts for generations. We believe that understanding our past is key to shaping our future."

Liam's eyes lit up with excitement. "This is exactly what we've been looking for. There's so much we can learn from these texts." It is here that they meet up again with Vivi, who had come aboard the sea train when no one was looking and once more offered her assistance to them and their journey.

The Exchange with Captain David

Later, they gathered in the Sea Train's main chamber, where David explained their next steps. "The Sea Train can take you to places that were once thought unreachable," he said. "But your journey will not be without challenges. There are still many dangers in the depths, in the air, and on other islands, and those secrets are well guarded."

Theo leaned forward, his excitement palpable. "We're ready for whatever comes our way. We've faced dangers before, and we're prepared to do it again."

David nodded. "I have no doubt of your courage and determination. We will stand by your side and offer our assistance in any way we can."

Liam exchanged a determined glance with his friends. "We've come this far, and we're not turning back now. We're ready to face whatever trials await us."

David smiled proudly. "Then let us begin. The Sea Train will take us to the Island of Mysteries first, and from there, your true test will begin." Captain David continued: "Before all that, we need to travel through the sacred caves and resupply the sea train at the underwater city. Princess Vivi will help us make that journey. Let's begin."

Vivi was radiant as ever, with her silver scales and vibrant green eyes. She greeted them all warmly and once again offered her support.

"I'm here to help you navigate the challenges ahead," Vivi said. "My knowledge of the ancient texts and the path to the sacred caves will be invaluable."

Ava smiled. "Thank you, Princess Vivi. We're grateful for your guidance."

Chapter XXIII:
The Journey to the Sacred Caves

With the guidance of Captain David and the crew, the Sea Train embarked on its journey to the sacred caves. The underwater landscape was breathtaking, with vibrant coral reefs, mysterious shipwrecks, and an abundance of marine life.

As they traveled, the crew shared stories of their own adventures and the history of the Sea Train. They spoke of the ancient civilization's rise and fall, their technological marvels, and the enduring legacy they left behind.

Kai, with his infectious enthusiasm, recounted tales of daring escapes and thrilling discoveries. "The ocean is full of wonders and mysteries," he said. "Every journey brings something new and exciting."

Rylan and Talia shared their knowledge of the Sea Train's mechanics and the challenges of navigating the deep. "It takes a lot of skill and precision to keep everything running smoothly," Rylan said. "But it's worth it to explore these incredible places."

Lyra and Nereus delved into the more esoteric aspects of the ancient civilization, discussing their beliefs, rituals, and the profound connection they had with the ocean. "They viewed the sea as both a source of life and a great mystery," Lyra explained. "Their respect for the ocean is evident in everything they created."

The Sacred Caves

After several hours of travel, the Sea Train arrived at the entrance to the sacred caves. The entrance was marked by towering stone pillars covered in ancient symbols and glowing crystals. The water around the entrance was calm and clear, creating a sense of serenity and anticipation.

With Vivi leading the way, the group entered the sacred caves. The air was filled with a sense of ancient power, and the walls were adorned with glowing crystals and intricate carvings that depicted the history and achievements of the ancient civilization.

The path through the caves was winding and filled with challenges. They encountered puzzles that required both intellect and intuition to solve, as well as trials that tested their physical and mental endurance. Each challenge brought them closer together, strengthening their bond and deepening their understanding of the ancient civilization.

At one point, they faced a guardian creature, a formidable being made of stone and magic. Theo and Emma fought bravely, using their skills and teamwork to overcome the guardian (the Sea Train defenses helped them on this formidable task). Liam and Ava deciphered ancient runes that revealed the creature's weaknesses, allowing them to defeat it and continue their journey. After hours of navigating the caves and overcoming numerous trials, they reached the underwater city. The sight of the city was more spectacular than when they where here the first time.

The Final Secret

As the vessel entered the city, a soft, golden light emerged from the temple that was opposite the ruler's palace. The five of them, Liam, Theo, Emma, Ava, and Vivi, left the sea train and its crew to resupply the sea train with all that was needed for the voyage ahead and made their way to the temple. Inside the temple, there was a chamber as vast as the main chamber where the ruler of the city saw visitors, filled with a soft, golden light. At the center of the chamber stood a pedestal, upon which lay a crystal orb.

Vivi approached the pedestal and placed her hand on the orb. "This is the Heart of the Ocean," she said, her voice filled with reverence. "It holds the final secrets of the Sea Train and the ancient civilization."

As she spoke, the orb began to glow, and images appeared in the air around them. They saw visions of the ancient civilization at its peak, their achievements, their connection to the ocean, and their eventual decline. The images revealed the true purpose of the Sea Train: to preserve their knowledge and legacy for future generations.

Liam, Ava, Emma, and Theo watched in awe, understanding the profound responsibility they now held. They had uncovered the secrets of the Sea Train and the ancient civilization, and it was up to them to honor and protect that legacy.

A New Beginning

As the visions faded, Vivi turned to the group. "You have proven yourselves worthy. The knowledge and legacy of the ancient civilization are now yours to safeguard and share."

Liam nodded, his voice filled with determination. "We will honor this responsibility. We will use this knowledge to make the world a better place and to preserve the legacy of the ancient civilization."

Ava, Emma, and Theo agreed, their hearts filled with pride and purpose. They had come a long way and faced countless challenges, but their journey had only just begun.

With the Heart of the Ocean and the secrets of the Sea Train, they set out on a new adventure, ready to explore the world and uncover its hidden wonders. The Sea Train awaited them, a symbol of their journey and their commitment to the future.

As they emerged from the temple and boarded the Sea Train once more, they felt a renewed sense of purpose and excitement. The world was vast and full of mysteries, and they were ready to explore every corner of it.

Together, they would honor the legacy of the ancient civilization and pave the way for a future filled with discovery and wonder. The adventure continued, and Liam, Ava, Emma, and Theo were ready to embrace it with open hearts and minds.

Return to Dave's Landing, final preparations and goodbyes.

Liam, Ava, Emma, and Theo, the princess and the crew of the sea train, leave the underwater city for Dave's landing. The guys wanted to see their parents before embarking on their next adventure. The people of Dave's landing and the kids' parents were lost for words when they set their eyes on the vessel and the crew but welcomed them all with open hands and love.

Over the next few weeks, Liam, Ava, Emma, and Theo immersed themselves in their new roles. Each day brought new lessons and experiences. Marina taught them how to read the stars and navigate the treacherous waters, her wisdom and patience guiding them through the intricacies of seafaring. Balthazar put them through rigorous training sessions, honing their combat skills and teaching them the art of strategy and defense. Zephyr shows them more about the inner workings of the Sea Train and how to operate and maintain the complex machinery that powered the vessel.

As they trained, they also bonded with the crew. They shared meals, stories, and laughter, forging friendships that would prove invaluable in the trials ahead. The crew admired the champions' determination and quickly grew to respect their leadership.

The Next Adventure

Finally, the day comes when they set out on their greatest adventure. Armed with maps, supplies, and their unbreakable bond, they journey into the unknown. Along the way, they discover not only physical treasures but also the more profound treasure of their friendship and personal growth. Through this journey, they come of age, maturing into the individuals they were always meant to be. Their adventures shape their identities, solidifying their roles within the group and in the world.

Each character managed to find their place and role within the group. Liam's leadership, Emma's intellect, Theo's strength, and Ava's empathy all contribute to their success. They face and overcome their ultimate challenge, a formidable obstacle that tests their unity and individual strengths to the limit.

With the Sea Train ready, the group prepared for the next leg of their journey. They knew that the path ahead would be filled with challenges, but they were prepared to face them together. The bonds they had forged through their trials were more robust than ever, and their shared purpose gave them the strength to move forward. They gave the orders, and the crew sprang into action, preparing the Sea Train for departure.

As the Sea Train began to move, its tracks humming with energy, the group felt a sense of exhilaration and anticipation. The Sea Train cut through the waves, and the tension on board was palpable. They knew that this was just the beginning of their journey and that many challenges lay ahead. The adventure continued, with the Sea Train guiding them through the hidden wonders of the ancient civilization. They were explorers, scholars, and adventurers, united by their quest for knowledge and discovery.

As they ventured into the unknown, the world stretched out before them, filled with endless possibilities and uncharted territories. Liam, Ava, Emma, and Theo were ready to face whatever challenges lay ahead, their hearts filled with the thrill of adventure and the promise of discovery.

Conclusion

Reflecting on their journey, they realize the profound impact it has had on their lives. They have grown not just as individuals but as a tight-knit group bound by shared experiences and mutual respect. They know their journey is far from over, with many more adventures awaiting them. Their story is one of dreams, adventure, treasure, and, most importantly, the unbreakable bond of friendship.